The Doomsday Marshal
and the Mountain Man

The Doomsday Marshal
and the
Mountain Man

RAY HOGAN

A Double D Western
DOUBLEDAY
New York *London* *Toronto* *Sydney* *Auckland*

A Double D Western
PUBLISHED BY DOUBLEDAY
a division of Bantam Doubleday Dell Publishing Group, Inc.
1540 Broadway, New York, New York 10036

Double D Western, Doubleday,
and the portrayal of the letters DD
are trademarks of Doubleday, a division of
Bantam Doubleday Dell Publishing Group, Inc.

Library of Congress Cataloging-in-Publication Data

Hogan, Ray, 1908–
The doomsday marshal and the mountain man/Ray Hogan.—1st ed.
    p.   cm.—(A Double D western)
1. Frontier and pioneer life—Fiction.   2. Kiowa Indians—Fiction.   I. Title.
II. Title: Doomsday marshal and the mountain man.
PS3558.O3473D633   1993
813'.54—dc20   92-46306
CIP

ISBN 0-385-46804-0
Copyright © 1993 by Ray Hogan
All Rights Reserved
Printed in the United States of America
September 1993
First Edition

10   9   8   7   6   5   4   3   2   1

to . . .
My beloved wife, Lois, who
went through hell with me

The Doomsday Marshal
and the Mountain Man

One

JOHN RYE, the famed Doomsday Marshal, moved slowly and silently through the thick oak brush and ghostly aspen trees to where he could get a better look at the ramshackle structure housing Brimtown's only saloon. He paused, touched the butt of the heavy pistol hanging at his hip to assure himself of its presence. Satisfied, he continued a few more steps. Again the lawman halted. A tight smile pulled at his thin lips as he got a closer view of the weathered old building. Hode Wilkinson's white gelding was standing at the hitch rack along with a half-dozen other horses.

A deep sigh escaped the marshal's throat. The long hunt for Wilkinson—called One Ear by the Indians—was finally over. Rye had been searching for the big mountain man for months—since the day he had received orders from his chief to track down and bring in the outlaw who had successfully defied the law for years.

Wanted for several murders and many other crimes, Wilkinson had become something of a legend to many in the area due to his boast that no lawman had the ability or the courage to capture him, and that if somehow one did manage it, no jail would be strong enough to hold him.

A giant of a man, said to be at least seven feet in height and weighing near three hundred pounds, he possessed the strength of several men coupled with the knowledge and ways of the Indians that served him well as he roamed the mountains of New Mexico and Colorado. He was a merciless man, and as cold-blooded and cruel as any human could be; it was imperative that he be brought in to face trial and the hangman. Rye's superior had stated such in the telegram he'd sent the marshal; Hode Wilkinson was making a mockery of the law, and he had to be stopped before other outlaws got the idea they could get away with ignoring it.

Hode lived somewhere in the high mountain country, either in the New Mexico or the Colorado area. No one seemed to know, or wanted to know the lawman suspected, just exactly which. It wasn't healthy to take an interest in Wilkinson. It was said that any man who did very likely would end up lying dead along one of the trails that laced the mountain or scarred the flat land spreading out below.

Rye came to attention. Two men came out of the saloon's front entrance and halted on its small wooden landing. The marshal studied them critically in the afternoon light. Both were familiar. One, a short, dark-skinned man, was named Thiebold. He was wanted in Texas for murder. The other, dressed in a checked suit and wearing a black derby hat, was a gambler known as Stud Allison. He too was a fugitive from Texas where he was wanted for gunning down a rancher in the aftermath of a card game.

Rye felt a twinge of conscience as he watched the men turn to their horses, mount up and ride off. Ordinarily he would have arrested the outlaws where they stood and either turned them over to the nearest sheriff or town marshal, or perhaps even taken them personally back to Texas, but he had to forgo that procedure in this instance. He had finally caught up with Wilkinson, who was wanted for not one or two murders, but for nine if the Kiowa Indian girl he had kidnapped after killing her mother and father was still alive. In all likelihood she was not.

Prior to that the outlaw had stopped a family on the Santa Fe Trail. They were on their way to Utah. He had slain the man and his wife as well as their son, taken what he found of value and left their wagon standing a short way off the well-traveled route. Another party of pilgrims noted the absence of life around the canvas-topped vehicle and investigated. Shocked by what they found, they had taken the victims and their wagon on west to Fort Union where they had turned the luckless party over to the army.

It was their deaths that brought John Rye into the picture. The army commandant had notified Washington headquarters, and they in turn had referred the matter to the chief U.S. Marshal. About the same time, in the settlement of Springtown, lying in the mountain country of northern New Mexico, Wilkinson was seen attempting to sell certain items that undoubtedly had come from some pilgrim's wagon. The officer leading an army patrol which happened to be in the town that day was persuaded to investigate.

The elderly lieutenant put two and two together and determined it was Wilkinson who had murdered the Utah-bound pilgrims. Since it was a civilian matter, he put him in the Springtown jail in the care of the settlement's lawman, Ben Jacklin. Later the outlaw, who brazenly admitted to the murders, was to be taken to Cimarron, a much larger town to the south where he would stand trial.

That never came to pass. Hode Wilkinson, true to his boasting, escaped after tricking the man Jacklin had hired as a jailer to watch over him while the lawman was at home catching up on his sleep.

Wilkinson made a clean getaway, turned east in his flight, coming upon a Kiowa village where he abducted an Indian girl named Morning Sky after killing her mother and father. He dropped from sight then, but a month or so later was seen back in his customary haunts. When he turned up in Brimtown a whiskey peddler had spotted him and passed the word on to the sheriff in Cimarron. He, in turn, had notified the chief marshal in faraway Washington who had immediately brought in John Rye.

Rye was a special lawman appointed originally by President Rutherford Hayes, with the authority to go anywhere in the country to arrest and bring in for trial any outlaw who was deemed dangerous enough to warrant his attention. A cool, completely controlled man, he was known for his ability to handle any situation involving outlaws. Considered cruel by many, he did only what was necessary to bring to justice a tough, ruthless criminal.

Tall for his time, six foot or so in height, usually weighing around two hundred pounds, he was all bone and hard muscle. With gray-blue eyes, he had dark, somewhat curly hair, heavy brows and a full mustache that partly concealed the stern, unyielding set of his mouth. In the Confederate cavalry during the war he was successively, after hostilities concluded, a hired gunman, bounty hunter, town marshal, ore wagon guard, sheriff's deputy and finally a Special U.S. Marshal.

A deadly, friendless type of man, he was a loner in every sense of the term, and one of few words. Now well known along the frontier, he was both feared and admired, and while he never cared for the descriptive title of Doomsday

Marshal that was applied to him, he never objected to it either, realizing that it had an intimidating effect on many outlaws which made his job easier.

Dressed in a gray, shield-style shirt, cord pants, stovepipe boots with army spurs, and dark, flat-crowned hat, he looked little different from most of the men coursing the West—a fact that he felt was all to his advantage.

"You sure ain't what I was expecting," Town Marshal Ben Jacklin had said that morning when Rye rode into Springtown and presented himself.

Rye shrugged. "Just what were you looking for?" he asked dryly.

A man lounging in the lawman's office laughed. "Well, for one thing you sure ain't big enough to go after old One Ear."

"Never bothered much about size," Rye said. "I carry a .45 Colt that equalizes things."

"Ain't going to help you much with Wilkinson," Jacklin said. Resentment toward the man who had been sent in to do the job at which he had failed showed plainly on Jacklin's narrow features. About thirty years of age, he was as tall as Rye but weighed less. He wore ordinary cowhand clothing and carried two bone-handled guns.

"Got my doubts that a couple of .45 slugs won't ever stop old Hode," he said indifferently. "Ain't never nobody been a match for him—not even the army. Tried to talk them into taking him in but they said no—that it wasn't an army matter. I figure they knew what they'd be up against and didn't want any part of it."

The man sitting in the chair tipped back against the wall, shook his head. "I don't mean no disrespect, Marshal. I've been told plenty about you—that you ain't the kind to back off from anything, but I'm scared you're headed for a trip to the boneyard if you go after Wilkinson alone."

Rye smiled faintly. "I've gone up against his kind before and I'm still on my feet. Either one of you got an idea where I can find him?"

"Ain't nobody can answer that," Jacklin said. "He holes up somewhere along the top of Red Mountain— some say on the New Mexico side, others say Colorado. Got a hideout cabin nobody ain't never seen."

"Got that little Indian gal he stole with him there, too, so they say," the man sprawled in the chair said. "Reckon that's the reason he ain't around much. Spends his time looking after her."

"Ain't no use asking anybody else where his cabin is," Jacklin said. "Either they don't know or won't say if they do. Best thing you can do is go hang around Brimtown. He shows up there once in a while."

"Brimtown," Rye echoed. "Expect that's what I'll do. Where is it?"

"At the foot of Red Mountain. Just take the trail north out of here. It'll take you right to it. I—" Jacklin paused, glanced out into the dusty street. Several cowhands laughing and talking noisily were riding by. The lawman eyed them critically until they were beyond his view. "Was about to say I can't give you no help. Got a bunch of trail drivers in town. If I don't stay right on their backs they'll take the place apart."

"No help necessary," Rye said laconically.

The man in the chair rocked forward in surprise. "You mean you're going after Hode Wilkinson alone?"

The marshal nodded. "Always found working alone at a time like this the best. I don't have to worry about some greenhorn posse member getting hurt."

"But good hell, man! This here's Hode Wilkinson

you're talking about going after. He's maybe killed a dozen men. Could be more. He ain't only bigger than all get-out, but meaner than a corn-cobbed tomcat. You won't stand—"

"I'll get him and I'll take him to Cimarron—either dead or alive. That'll be up to him," Rye said in his quiet way.

Jacklin slid a sly glance at the man in the chair and smiled. "Well, I guess you know what you're doing," he said, sarcasm coloring his voice, "but your reputation ain't going to do you no good when you try to take in Hode."

"Something I never depend on," Rye said, and turned and left the town marshal's office.

The lawman watched the two outlaws who had come out of the saloon—the PROSPECTOR, a faded, bullet-marked sign high on the building's false front advised—until they had disappeared beyond a bend in the trail, and then put his attention back upon the old building. The tip the Cimarron sheriff had furnished, that Wilkinson was back in his old haunts, had been good. Rye had hung around Brimtown, keeping well out of sight, for three days when the big outlaw had shown up. Utterly confident, Hode had come down off the mountain, making no effort to hide his movements as he left the trail and followed the short street to the saloon.

Rye shifted his attention to the bay gelding that he now rode in place of the chestnut that had been his favorite for years but was now retired to a farm in Missouri, and saw that the horse was where he had left him. Turning toward the bay, he hesitated briefly as a sudden fluttering sound followed by the soft whisper of wings broke the quiet. A bird of some sort, startled by his appearance, launched itself into frantic flight. Rye grinned wryly and continued.

Taking up the gelding's reins, he led him to the hitch
rack. After tying him to the crossbar a bit to one side of
Wilkinson's white, he pulled the 10-gauge shotgun from
the saddle scabbard and headed for the entrance of the
Prospector. There would be at least three more men in the
saloon besides Hode Wilkinson, judging from the trio of
horses remaining at the rack. No doubt they also were
outlaws. Such would complicate matters considerably.
Rye gave that thought, and then shrugged and walked on
in the fading afternoon light.

Two

RYE HALTED at the entrance to the saloon, and in a swift, surveying glance, took in the dimly lit place and its contents. A somewhat small, square room with an open ceiling and bare walls, it contained a few tables and chairs, a bar constructed of waist-high sawhorses and two-inch-thick planks laid across them, and a shelf affixed to the wall behind.

There was no mirror, nor decorations of any kind, and the light, poor at its best, was furnished by a single high window and a half-dozen oil lamps placed at various locations around the room. Brass cuspidors were conspicuous by their absence, but patrons were provided the luxury of small sandboxes available at several points.

The marshal spotted Hode Wilkinson immediately; the outlaw's hulking size made it impossible not to do so. He stood alone at the crude counter. The bartender, a squat, dark-haired man with a curving, full mustache and scraggly beard to match, wearing a black sateen shirt, denim pants and a white apron badly in need of washing, dozed against the sparsely stocked shelf.

Neither Wilkinson nor the bartender had noticed Rye's

presence in the doorway, and taking advantage of that fact, the lawman considered the outlaw. Every bit as large as had been said, Wilkinson was dressed in deerskin pants, wore moccasins and a once blue undershirt that clung tightly to his muscular body.

No hat covered the thick, ragged blond hair that crowned his head, and from the side, his mustache and beard, both dark, appeared stained and unkempt. A lever action rifle was propped against the sawhorse near his right leg and a long skinning knife hung from a rope belt around his waist.

Where were the three riders of the horses standing at the hitch rack?

Rye's features tightened as he turned his attention to the rest of the evil-smelling room. They were nowhere to be seen and that set up a disturbance in John Rye's mind. In a situation such as this every factor had to be accounted for. There were two doors in the rear wall of the building. One probably led to the outside, he reckoned, the other to a room most likely used for sleeping or possibly private card games. If that was where the missing men were, and they remained there, they would pose no problem. Rye swore silently. He was not one to take anything for granted, but to delay longer would be dangerous. Shotgun hanging in the crook of his left arm, right hand hovering near the .45 on his hip, he entered the saloon and slanted across the sawdust-covered floor toward Hode Wilkinson.

The bartender glanced up as the lawman approached. Rye shook his head in silent warning but Wilkinson, possessing that inner warning device common to men who live on the edge, started to wheel.

"Don't!" Rye snapped, closing in quickly. "I'm a United States Marshal and I've got a 10-gauge, double-barreled shotgun loaded with buckshot pointed at your back. You do what I tell you or I'll blow you in two!"

Wilkinson froze. "What—" he began, but Rye cut him off.

"I'm arresting you for jailbreak and for murder. I'm taking you back to—"

Wilkinson's massive shoulders stirred indifferently. "Maybe," he said in a slightly accented voice. "Ain't nobody yet ever took me—"

"Different this time," Rye said coolly, pulling the skinning knife from Hode's belt and tossing it into the corner beyond the bar. "Put your hands behind you."

Hode complied slowly. Rye, the muzzle of the 10 gauge jammed hard against the outlaw's spine, took the chain-connected steel cuffs from his pocket and snapped them about the outlaw's wrists, then stepped back. He nodded to the bartender and then the side entrance.

"That door unlocked?"

"I reckon it is," the man behind the counter replied. His face was taut with anger and hostility and hate glowed in his eyes.

"You ain't getting far with me," Wilkinson growled. "I've been caught by better badge-toters than you, bigger ones, too, and they didn't never get me nowhere. And when I bust loose, I aim to kill you—I'm making you that promise."

"Been plenty tried it," Rye said mildly. "Now turn around and head for that side door."

Rye had chosen that route simply because it would put them closer to the horses. He knew he had no ordinary prisoner here in Hode Wilkinson. He would have to take every precaution if he was to get him back to Springtown or Cimarron alive.

Hode wheeled slowly in the taut silence, shaking his

shaggy head like some huge, cornered animal. He spat, started for the doorway. Rye, shotgun still pushing against the outlaw's back while he maintained a safe distance should Hode whirl and attempt to knock the weapon aside, drew his .45 with his free hand.

"You hang on to my knife and rifle," Wilkinson called over his shoulder to the bartender. "I'll be coming back for them."

Rye ignored the aside. He prodded the outlaw harder with the shotgun. "Out that door and cut left," he said. "When we get to the horses hold up. I aim to put a rope around your neck so you won't be trying to make a run for it."

"You're a'pointing that damn scattergun at me—ain't that enough? Or maybe you're a mite scared I'll—"

"Not that," Rye said evenly. "I'd as soon kill you as not. Be easier to take you in. But my orders are to bring you in alive so's they can hang you."

Hode, shuffling along slowly, again wagged his head. "Won't never come to no hanging. I'll—"

"What's going on here, Otey?"

At the sound of the question Rye stepped quickly to one side to face the three men who had come from the back, still holding the shotgun on Wilkinson. He had gambled on the trio posing no interference but it hadn't worked out.

"This here marshal's aiming to take the big fellow, name's Hode Wilkinson, in for a hanging."

"All by himself?" one of the men said in a bantering tone. "Sure must figure hisself for one hell of a man. If—"

"Keep out of this!" Rye cut in harshly. "I'm a U.S. Marshal! Don't interfere."

"Yeh, I reckon you are," a second man said. "You're the one they call the Doomsday Marshal 'cause you're such a hardcase. You ought to recollect me. I'm Charlie Vickers."

Vickers . . . Rye, angry at the turn of luck, nodded. In the tight silence that gripped the room he was motionless, the shotgun still leveled at Wilkinson, his .45 turned in the direction of the three men now standing at the end of the bar.

"I remember you," he said finally. "Turned you over to the law in Tucson for holding up a stage and shooting one of the passengers."

"And for doing that, the damn judge put me in Yuma prison for three years, where I done nothing but bust rocks. Swore I'd get even with you if ever I got the chance."

"Forget it," Rye said coldly.

"Nope, ain't about to—fact is I ain't never going to forget about that sweatbox and who sent me there. This here's my chance, and I got a couple of friends along. Both was with me in Yuma and they're feeling the same about you as I do, you being a lousy lawman."

Rye's cold eyes settled on the two men with Vickers. One he recognized as Red McHugh—a face he'd seen on wanted posters. A cattle rustler. The other man, short in stature and with the loose slouch of a gunman, was a stranger.

"Expect you know Red. He's been around for a spell. Other gent is Abilene Pierce. He's sort of well known, too."

Vickers had moved in a few steps closer to the bar. Lamplight now fell upon him affording the lawman a better look. He was much thinner and darker than Rye remembered, but a term in Yuma prison wrought big changes in any man.

Rye shook his head. "Best you think about this. You're

all out of Yuma. Be smart and don't start something that will put you behind bars again—or maybe get you killed."

Vickers laughed. "You hear that, boys? Now, he's a real tough one, ain't he—tough talking, anyway. Him standing there with that big galoot of a stranger and the three of us just a'honing to fill him plumb full of holes. Spread out boys, let's—"

Rye triggered his .45 and instantly sent a bullet into Vickers before the outlaw could finish his words. At the same instant Pierce and McHugh fired their weapons but Rye was moving away. From the corner of an eye he saw Otey, the bartender, a rifle in his hands, straighten up. The lawman snapped a shot at him, felt the shotgun he was holding against Hode Wilkinson fly out of his hands as the big man knocked it aside and lunged for the door.

Smoke boiling about him, changing the smells in the room from stale, spilled whiskey to gunpowder, Rye rocked to one side and aimed a shot at Wilkinson just as Red McHugh fired. The bullet ripped through the slack in the sleeve of his shirt and buried itself in the wall beyond him. Spinning, Rye threw a quick, deadly bullet at McHugh, saw him stagger and start to fall. Instantly he swung his attention back to Wilkinson.

Through the haze he saw the mountain man had reached the door and twisted about so he could trip the latch. In the next moment he was stumbling into the open. Rye started to follow but dodged to one side as Pierce fired and yelled.

"Damn you, you stinking lawdog! You've done killed my two pards! I—"

Rye, on one knee, triggered his weapon. Pierce jolted from the impact of the heavy bullet, half turned, caught his balance and fell to the floor. Outside, in that same moment, the sudden hammer of a horse moving off fast reached him. He swore deeply and wheeled to Otey.

"How about it, bartender?" he demanded, fury riding his words. "You want to be the fourth man down?"

Otey dropped the rifle and hurriedly raised his hands. "No, sir! I don't want none of this!" he yelled.

"Well, you sure as hell've got it coming!" Rye said. "You were aiming to cut me down with that rifle."

"I—I sure don't know what I was thinking of, Marshal —I sure don't unless one of them outlaws was pointing his gun at me."

The last was a pure lie but Rye made no comment. He crossed to the door and looked out. Wilkinson's horse, of course, was gone. Rye swore as he reloaded his gun. It had been a long time since he'd lost a prisoner, so long in fact that he couldn't recall when it had happened.

"Marshal, are you going to shoot me—or take me in?" he heard the bartender ask in a plaintive voice.

Three

RYE DROPPED his reloaded gun back into its holster. There was no need to retrieve the shotgun; he could see from where he stood that the stock had been splintered when it struck the wall.

"No, not unless you get in my way again," he answered. Smoke still clung to the ceiling of the saloon and the smell of cordite overrode all other odors. "You bury these men and we'll call it square . . . You know Wilkinson?"

"Can't say as I do," the bartender said, shrugging. "Nobody else does either. Comes in here maybe two or three times a month, maybe less. Always alone. I reckon he ain't got no friends. I—I want to tell you again, Marshal, I didn't know who you was."

The cold, level anger that had filled John Rye was finally beginning to subside. "You heard me tell Wilkinson, didn't you?"

"Well, yes, reckon I did."

"Same goes for those outlaws. Way it shapes up you were interfering with the law, and you damn well knew it!" Rye's low voice still had an edge to it. Losing a prisoner was like shooting yourself in the foot—only worse. "You know where Wilkinson's cabin is?"

Rye moved in a few steps as he spoke, picked up Hode's rifle and laid it on the counter. He should keep it as a replacement for his shattered shotgun, he thought, but he never liked the idea of using another man's gun. An unfamiliar weapon with untrue sights or some other defect could get you killed.

"Sure don't, Marshal, and that's the God's truth! Back up on the mountain, I've heard, but don't nobody seem to know just where . . . I sure ain't looking forward to digging graves for them stiffs—"

"Then load them up on their horses and take them in to the marshal in Springtown. Name's Jacklin."

Otey's face sagged. "I do that and he'll throw me in jail. Me and him's had dealings before."

"Skip telling him you had a part in the shooting. Can just say they tried to gun me down while I was taking in Wilkinson."

The bartender brightened. "Thanks, Marshal. You know if there's a reward out for any of them three?"

"Expect there is," Rye said, turning for the door. Wilkinson had apparently headed up the mountain, taking the fairly well-marked trail that Rye had noted earlier. "Collecting it will be up to you. Just you tell Jacklin what I said."

"Sure, sure. You be coming back this way?"

"Most likely," the lawman replied, and stepped out into the fading day.

It would soon be too dark to trail Hode Wilkinson, he realized, but the outlaw had gone up the trail—that much he knew for certain. He would go as far as possible, until he could no longer see any signs, and then halt and wait for daylight. Too, he might get lucky; Wilkinson might come back down the trail with the thought in mind of getting a shot at him.

Rye paused, glanced back through the open door of the saloon. The bartender was crouched over the body of Charlie Vickers. He was going through the outlaw's pockets. Rye shrugged and turned away. He supposed there was nothing wrong with that inasmuch as he'd handed the dead outlaws over to Otey, but it did send a wave of disgust through the marshal.

One of his final recollections of the war was of a battle-field where Union and Confederate troops had waged a hard-fought battle. A number of ghoulish camp followers were ransacking the bodies of the men who had been killed in the engagement. A close friend of Rye's had been one of those who had fallen.

Brushing aside the memory, the lawman strode purposely on to where his horse waited. Hode Wilkinson was somewhere up on the mountain, and the long, hard task of digging the killer out and taking him back to face justice was beginning all over again. He'd had Wilkinson there in his hands in the saloon and but for a bit of bad luck, he'd now be on his way that very moment for Springtown with the big mountain man.

Rye shrugged as he pulled the leathers loose from the crossbar of the rack and swung up into the saddle of the bay. There was nothing to be gained by rehashing what had happened; it was done and nothing in the world could change it. The one thing left was to track down Hode Wilkinson, put him in irons again and take him to jail.

Cutting the bay about in the near dark, Rye headed for the foot of the trail. He pulled up short as he felt the round, hard muzzle of a rifle dig into his side. Wilkinson?

Cursing his own carelessness in not looking around, he raised his hands slowly and turned to his right.

It wasn't Hode Wilkinson but a young Indian. The brave, face stolid, eyes narrowed with hatred, stared at him silently. A second brave of probably the same age materialized from the brush nearby. He, too, had a rifle in his hands, and was leveling it at the lawman.

"What the hell do you want?" Rye demanded harshly. His patience at being interfered with had come to an abrupt end.

"One Ear," the brave nearest him answered.

It was Hode Wilkinson they were after. Most likely they were from the village that Wilkinson had kidnapped the girl from. He shook his head and started to speak. At that the Indian pressing the rifle muzzle into his ribs jabbed him viciously. Anger flared through Rye.

"I don't have him—can't you see that?"

The second brave now stood directly in front of the lawman and said something in his native tongue to his partner. Rye felt the pressure of the rifle barrel lessen.

"We were told you have come to take One Ear to a white man's prison," the second brave said in fairly good English.

"My job!" Rye snapped.

"But you do not make him your prisoner?"

Rye jerked a thumb at the saloon. The side door was now closed. "Had him, but ran into a bit of trouble. He got away. Expect you're looking for him, too."

"It is so. I am called Wolf Killer. I am a Kiowa, the son of Spotted Antelope, who was killed by One Ear. He also carried away my sister, Morning Sky."

"I am Brown Bear," the second brave said before Rye could speak. "Morning Sky was to be my woman—my

wife as you would say. We have hunted One Ear since the
night he did these bad things. What are you called?"

"John Rye. I am a lawman—a United States Marshal."

"We know of you," Wolf Killer said. "It is told you are
of good deeds. When we hear that you are in this part of
the country to capture One Ear, we were glad for we felt
sure you would hand him to us and the Kiowas could
make him pay for what he had done to us."

Rye made no comment, but realized that he now faced
not only the task of capturing Wilkinson but keeping the
big mountain man out of the vengeful hands of the Kiowas. He glanced about. Brown Bear had moved a few
steps away from the restless bay, and Wolf Killer had also
withdrawn slightly. The lawman braced himself. He could
in no way have the two Kiowas tagging along with him
while he continued to search for Wilkinson. Such would
only lead to serious trouble, but he would like to avoid
any bloodshed where they were concerned, if possible.

"You go to Springtown," he said, settling himself in the
saddle. "I will come there later." At that point Rye drove
his spurs into the flanks of the nervous bay.

The horse lunged forward at the unexpected jab of the
spurs. Wolf Killer threw himself out of the horse's path.
From the corner of an eye the lawman saw Brown Bear
jerk back and whip up his rifle. Rye heard Wolf Killer yell
something, and bent low in the saddle to offer as small a
target as possible for the young Kiowa. Likely Wolf Killer
was warning his partner not to shoot as he was their only
lead to Wilkinson, but Rye was assuming nothing.

In the next moment the bay shied wildly. Rye had a
glimpse of a third brave coming out of the dense growth.
The Indian made a grab and caught the bridle of the bay
in his left hand while he slashed at Rye with the knife he

held in his right. The blade missed but the weight of the brave clinging onto the bridle brought the bay to his knees. Rye cursed as he left the saddle to keep from being caught under the falling horse. Nothing was going right for him—not a damn thing!

Four

RYE HIT THE GROUND on one shoulder, rolled quickly and came to his feet, gun in hand. He should have known there would be more than two Indians in the party. Like as not there yet were several hiding back in the brush. He wheeled, faced the one who called himself Brown Bear and the other, Wolf Killer. The third brave who had dragged down the bay was now standing beside them knife still clutched in his hand. The first two Kiowas were leveling their rifles at him. Nearby the bay was thrashing about as he struggled to come upright.

Rye shrugged, holstered his weapon, crossed his arms as a sign he would offer no resistance. It was still some time until dark and off in the trees to the south an owl hooted a greeting to the coming night.

"While you stop me the man we both want is getting away," the lawman said quietly.

There was no anger apparent in his voice but inwardly he was seething. First it was Charlie Vickers and his two friends, now it was a party of vengeance-seeking Kiowas. Who or what would be next?

"Do you know where he lives?" Brown Bear asked.

"Only thing I know is that he lives somewhere on this mountain," the lawman replied. "I trailed him to here. Now I am losing him."

"Other white men live on the mountain. They will tell you where to find his cabin." It was the newcomer, the third brave with the knife, who made the statement.

Rye nodded to him. "I see you speak my language, too. What you say has no meaning. If any knew, they would not say so because they fear the mountain man. I know the braves with you. What are you called?"

"I am Little Horse, the son of Gannok. We speak your language because the agent's woman taught us so."

"Are you blood brother to Wolf Killer and Brown Bear?"

"We are brothers because we are Kiowa and because we are of the same clan."

"Are there more of you in the brush?"

"No, there are but three of us."

Rye shook his head. "It is not good to have so many tracking this man you call One Ear. He will become suspicious and go into hiding again. You should not be here."

"I am Kiowa," Little Horse said with great dignity. "I come because the white men have again hurt my people."

"A white man—not all white men," Rye said. "That is why I hunt him. He has wronged white people, too."

Little Horse spat, said something to Wolf Killer in Kiowa. Both he and Brown Bear shook their heads.

"Are you afraid to speak my tongue?" Rye asked. He was so far behind Hode Wilkinson now that a few more minutes would not matter, especially if he could get the Kiowas off his back. "Do you fear that what you say is not the truth and I will know it?"

Little Horse spat again, this time angrily. "You speak of truth. It is something no white man lives by. They say they

are our friends but they have always been enemies of the
Indian people, killing them, driving them off their land,
destroying the buffalo and the antelope—"

"That was many years ago, and they were wrong to do
as they did. You cannot blame all white men for the bad
things a few did."

"There is no difference! White men have driven us to
where there is no hunting. They have killed many of our
people, stolen our young women or disgraced them by
force!"

The voice of Little Horse had risen, and his features
were distorted by anger, and even in the half light Rye
could see that his eyes glowed with a fierce hate.

"You judge all whites by a few," the lawman said, and
turned his attention to Brown Bear and Wolf Killer.

"The outlaw we seek gets farther away while we engage
in useless talk. Is it not best I go now and try to pick up his
trail?"

Little Horse smiled. He had strong, well-formed features, broad shoulders and the muscles of his torso were
visible cords beneath his copper skin.

"You will do much if you can track him in the dark—"

"It will not be the first time I have tried."

"I know you speak the truth but it will be a hard task,"
Wolf Killer said. "We cannot allow you to go. We must
keep you with us so that when we find One Ear he will
become our prisoner."

"My prisoner," Rye corrected in a flat, firm voice. "My
government will hang him for the crimes he has commit-
ted."

Little Horse again spat angrily. "The Kiowa people and
Kiowa law were here many years before the white man
came. It is the right of the Kiowas to punish this man."

"You are forgetting that in this time the white man's

law comes first," Rye said quietly. "It will see that justice is done for the Indian people as well as for the whites."

"Faw!" Little Horse shouted, waving a fist. He was an older man than Brown Bear and Wolf Killer and wore white cotton pants and a red dotted calico shirt—unlike his two companions who were clad only in breechcloths. "It is well known the word of a white man is without worth!"

Rye turned to the other braves. "I can't waste the night talking to Little Horse. His mind is closed. I am a patient man but I have none for him. Do you figure to tie me up and keep me here until daylight?"

Back up on the mountain a coyote barked, breaking the silence of the towering, tree-covered slope. Wolf Killer listened for a few moments and then nodded. "It is best. Even though we have great experience in tracking, we cannot do it in the dark which will soon be here."

"Wilkinson—One Ear as you call him—may get clean away if we wait till daylight. We should start now."

"Why must it always be the white man's way? It is the same with the law—the white man's law always must come first!" Little Horse declared. "Kiowa law is good. One Ear will suffer much for the evil he has done!"

"He'll die just the same under our law."

"But is it not true he will die quick and without having suffered for what he has done? Kiowa law will—"

"Torture him—that what you're trying to say? The white man's law doesn't believe in torture. It is felt that it is cruel and inhuman."

John Rye could not say so but there had been times when an outlaw he had arrested for a particularly brutal crime deserved extreme punishment such as the Indian people meted out. But those were thoughts he kept to him-

self; he was a representative of the white man's law and
had sworn to enforce and live by it.

"Is not what he has done inhuman and cruel? Can you
not see in your mind that the young girl who was to be
Brown Bear's woman in marriage is now suffering at the
hands of One Ear? Do you not think that my woman, who
he caught by the river one day and killed when he was
finished with her, did not suffer?"

Rye nodded. He had not known about Little Horse's
wife, but it was not difficult to understand the older
brave's bitterness.

"I am sorry for you and Brown Bear and I am ashamed
that a white man has wronged you both. Such makes it
most important that I find him and put him in chains."

"Will you kill him?" Wolf Killer asked.

Again the coyote somewhere high on a ridge or slope of
the Sangre de Cristos broke the mountain hush with its
discordant howl.

"Only if I have to," Rye said. "I was ordered by my
chief to bring him in alive. He will be hung as a lesson to
other outlaws."

Wolf Killer shook his head. "Then I fear we are to be
enemies."

"It is always so!" Little Horse shouted. "Who can say
for sure One Ear will be punished by the white man's law?
He will in some way escape like he has in the past—like he
has done this night!"

Rye glanced toward the trail. While all the useless
palavering, so dear to the Indian people, was going on,
Hode Wilkinson was getting farther away. True, his finding the outlaw in the darkness of a moonless and starless
night would likely be an impossibility unless pure luck
intervened, but he at least could be on the trail.

Unlike John Rye's usual attitude at such times, he was

reluctant to have a shootout with the braves. That he could put an end to the interminable talking was a certainty. The Kiowas were equipped only with rifles, and the long guns were far less maneuverable than his .45.

"I am sorry that we cannot be friends," Rye said, ignoring the comments of Little Horse, "but I was told to bring in this man for punishment. Aim to do just that."

"No!" Little Horse yelled, and snatching the rifle from Brown Bear's hand, leveled it at the lawman.

Rye drew fast. His .45 blasted the quiet, and set up a rolling chain of echoes. The bullet struck the rifle in Little Horse's hands, glanced off and buried itself in his shoulder. The brave staggered back as Wolf Killer grabbed for his rifle, propped against a bush at his side. Rye covered him instantly with his weapon and shook his head.

"No! I don't want to shoot you—either one of you— but I will if I have to. Little Horse gave me no choice."

Stepping forward slowly, he took up Wolf Killer's rifle, and then that of Brown Bear, and hung them under his arm. If Little Horse had a weapon other than his knife, it was nowhere to be seen.

"I will take your guns now," the marshal said. "I go north to find Wilkinson—One Ear. After a time you can follow. Your rifles will be on the trail." Crossing to where the bay gelding stood, he swung up into the saddle.

"Do not follow until it is full dark," he warned, and touching the horse with his spurs, he headed across the base of the mountain on a northerly course.

He did not know if the Indians had seen the outlaw leave. It was doubtful they had, otherwise they would have been in pursuit of the killer and not waiting in the brush for him.

Bearing north for a good fifty yards or so, Rye set as rapid a pace as the bay could manage on the narrow path cutting through the brush and trees. He glanced back as the trail cut to the right. Three dim figures were discernible, two of which appeared to be helping the third. He hadn't killed Little Horse and felt relief at that knowledge. He had nothing against the Kiowa braves but in no way was he about to let them interfere with the task he'd been assigned.

Waiting no longer, Rye dropped the rifles he was carrying onto the path where they would be easily found, and changing course, cut back for the main trail that led up the mountain.

Five

THE MOON AND STARS had finally come out, illuminating the silent land and lending an eerie aura to the slope. Pines stood tall and straight, without sound in the windless night, but the stark, white aspen's leaves trembled constantly as if time, skipping what was left of summer and ignoring fall, had placed them in winter's icy grasp.

Carefully threading his way through the impeding growth so as to avoid any undue noise, John Rye continued on a slanting course up the mountain. He should intersect the main trail shortly, he figured, unless he had misjudged and the route lay farther south. He doubted that, however. What little of it he had seen before the encounter in the saloon appeared to him to angle northerly.

Always a cautious man at such times, the lawman halted periodically to listen for sounds of pursuit. He was dealing with dangerous enemies now, he knew. The meeting with the Kiowas had been cool and wary in the beginning but the fact that the braves were as determined as he to lay Hode Wilkinson by the heels put them in exact opposition. His wounding of Little Horse during the escape would further intensify the bad blood between them. Little Horse now had a personal score to settle with him.

Rye reached the trail leading up the mountain an hour or so later. There he halted once more and took careful stock. The Indians may have split up, one of them, probably with their wounded member, continuing north on the easier trail he had followed, the remaining brave taking the other route.

After listening for a long five minutes and hearing nothing unusual, the lawman rode on, keeping to the edge of the trail as much as possible. Coyotes were now in full chorus, and down in the valley slowly taking shape below, a wolf made his presence known. Occasionally an owl hooted quietly in the spruce- and pine-scented night, and small animals rustled about in the dry leaves of the columbine, sedge and other low plants gathered by the wind. Twice he startled mule deer feeding in the little hollows and sent them bounding away in the silvered night.

It was great country, unbelievably beautiful in the pale moon and starlight and likely to be equally so during the daytime hours. Rye had often wondered what he would do when the time came to retire from his job as a Special U.S. Marshal—assuming he lived to see that day—and it occurred to him now that here would be ideal country in which to settle down, perhaps raise a few cattle and take it easy.

Could he do that? Could he ever give up a life of riding free across the frontier, the excitement of hunting down and capturing a dangerous outlaw who was always on the lookout for a chance to test his ability with a sixgun or a rifle? He always came to the conclusion that such would be an impossibility, that he could never give it up. He was born to be a lawman—and chances were he'd die a lawman.

Rye came to a halt. A wide, open place in the trail, one where loose soil had washed down from a higher place, lay before him. In the full light of the heavens it offered him his first opportunity to check for tracks. Dismounting, he dropped to a crouch and examined the soft earth. Satisfaction stirred through him. The hoofprints of a horse passing not too long ago were plain. It had to be Hode Wilkinson.

He glanced back down the slope. There were still no signs of the Kiowas but Rye knew he could put no trust in that. If on the trail, separately or together, they would be moving carefully and silently, employing every means to not be seen or heard. The Kiowas, he'd been told, were not among the best trackers of all the tribes, but that would count for little here; they had only to follow the trail, and when the light grew strong enough find where Wilkinson had turned off to get to his cabin.

It was up to him to get there first. He must locate that point and wipe it out. He should continue on for a distance on his own horse to lead the braves away from the turnoff, come to a halt in some confusing area where the Kiowas would lose the trail entirely.

Climbing back onto the bay, Rye rode on. The path was narrowing and the side of the mountain was becoming steeper and much nearer. He was riding along with the wall of a cliff on one side, a sheer drop-off into the valley on the other. It would be no place to meet with Hode Wilkinson, he thought grimly—or the Indians either for that matter.

Keeping the bay fairly close to the cliff in the event there was a soft shoulder or a washout on the opposite side, Rye looked down into the valley. In the pale light it appeared smooth with grass and low shrubs. Trees grew at irregular intervals, and cutting through the center of the swale was a winding, silver ribbon that marked a stream. Farther on, in a clearing, a single light glowed; a lamp in a window, no doubt. Whoever it was had a small piece of paradise, he thought.

Could it be Wilkinson's place? It was said to be well up on the mountain. If so it was not as well hidden as reported. Rye shook his head. That fact alone ruled out the possibility of it being the outlaw's home.

However, if the tracks of the horse petered out, he would need to get down into the valley and make certain one way or the other that it was or was not Wilkinson's cabin. He would continue on, though, until he was sure the outlaw was not ahead of him—a not too difficult task, as periodic moist places along the trail made it easy to see hoofprints.

He was no longer climbing, Rye realized. Either he was getting near the summit of the mountain, which seemed unlikely, or the trail was beginning to slope toward the floor of the valley. Too, it was wider and the rocky wall on his right had receded. Brush, rocks and a few small trees gradually replaced the cliff for a short distance, and then again the ragged wall reappeared.

The marshal looked ahead. Hode Wilkinson was still somewhere in front of him, as the tracks of his horse clearly indicated. And there were no signs that Wolf Killer and the other two braves were anywhere in the vicinity.

An uneasiness began to plague Rye, a feeling that it was all going too well, that something was about to happen. It was a premonition that occasionally possessed him when things were about to go wrong and disaster strike. Too many times the inner warning had proven true and he had long since learned to respect it.

More alert, he rode on, walking the bay, his attention swinging from side to side as well as back and forward. The feeling heightened. Something was not right, just what he could not put his finger on. There were no indications that Wilkinson was anywhere near. The same was true where the Kiowas were concerned. What then could be sounding the alarm within him?

The night was quiet except for the coyotes. Stars sparkled overhead, and the moon, now well on its way, shone brightly, glistening on the distant surface of the stream below, softening the ragged shapes of the brush and outlining the pines, spruces and aspen.

In that next fragment of time, Rye realized his intuition had not been wrong. At a brushy point near where the ragged cliff lifting up on his right began to take shape again, a huge figure came hurtling out of the heavy growth at him.

Rye knew instantly that it was Wilkinson. He made a grab for his gun—but there was no time. The bay, frightened by the dark shape lunging at him, shied wildly. The edge of the trail gave way and the big horse plunged over the side, carrying Rye with him. Fear, Wilkinson's great strength and the somewhat narrow section of the trail had been the horse's undoing.

Rye felt the weight of the bay come down on his left leg as the animal, hoofs flailing in thin air, began to tumble. Rye managed to kick clear. In that same instant he glimpsed Hode Wilkinson towering above him on the lip of the slope. And then all went black as his head struck a solid, unyielding mass of rock.

Six

JOHN RYE returned to consciousness with pain throbbing throughout his body, and the sweet sound of a woman's voice singing an old, familiar song in his ears. He lay quiet, eyes on the ceiling. After a few minutes he looked about.

He was in someone's cabin. The plastered log walls were white and clean. On one hung a calendar, a few paintings in ornate frames graced another, while the remaining two supported shelving. A curtained clothes closet was in one corner and near it a window permitted sunlight to enter the room. He was on a corn husk mattress with several piece quilts and a wool blanket spread over him.

Rye became aware that the quiet singing had ceased. He turned his head, flinching visibly at the pain, and looked to see where the singing had come from. A young woman in her early twenties was standing in a doorway smiling at him.

"It's nice to see you're back among the living," she said, coming into the room. Halting at the foot of the bed, she added, "Zeb and I wondered for a spell if you'd make it."

"Zeb?" the lawman repeated. He still was a bit groggy and the continued hammering of sullen pain was not making his return to full consciousness any faster.

"Zeb Oliver, my uncle. This is his cabin. My name is Dixie—it's really Annabelle but when Zeb brought me to live with him, he changed it to Dixie. Said Annabelle was too long a name. We figure you're a lawman from the papers you carry."

"Yes, name's John Rye. I'm a U.S. Marshal."

"And you came here after Hode Wilkinson."

Rye struggled to sit up, failed and lay back. "How did you know that? My papers never—"

Dixie shrugged. "Every lawman that comes through here is looking to arrest him. They all fail."

"Somebody didn't. He was in jail and broke out—"

"So we've been told. Whoever it was that did arrest him didn't do it around here. Was in some town east of here . . . You hungry?"

Rye shook his head carefully, waited a bit for the pain to subside. "How long have I been here?"

"Since early yesterday morning."

The lawman swore softly. Not only had Wilkinson had more than enough time to leave the area if he chose, but the Kiowas' chances of finding and capturing the outlaw were now much better.

"You sure you're not hungry? Expect you haven't had anything to eat for some time."

Rye studied the woman. She was pretty, had dark hair, blue eyes, an oval face and a bright, quick smile. Dressed in a faded but clean man's shirt, she also wore pants that had been cut down to fit—both articles no doubt once the property of the uncle she called Zeb.

"A cup of coffee would taste mighty good if you have it made. And I reckon I could use a little bread and meat."

"Now you do sound better! You were lucky that when your horse fell you didn't break a leg or something. Zeb went over you after we brought you here. He said he was sure you didn't have any broken bones."

"Sometimes you get lucky," Rye said. "I'm obliged to you both for looking after me."

Dixie smiled, turned and started for the adjoining room. "I'll get you the coffee now, then I'll fix you a bite to eat."

"I'll sure appreciate it," the lawman said and again made the effort to sit up. This time succeeding, he glanced about. His gear was piled in one corner of the room, holster and gun hanging from the horn of the saddle.

"My horse—" he began as Dixie returned with a large granite cup of coffee. "What about him?"

"The fall killed him," she replied, handing him the cup. "I'm sorry. Have you had him long?"

"Not long. He was a good horse . . . Are my clothes there in that wardrobe?"

"Most of them," Dixie said. "Your shirt and pants were in pretty bad shape from the rocks and brush. I cleaned and mended them."

"I'm obliged to you again," Rye said, sipping at the strong brew. "I'd like to pay you for your trouble."

"That's not necessary. We don't accept anything for helping folks," Dixie said stiffly, and lips tight, wheeled and left the room.

He should have known better, Rye thought, but he was only trying to express his appreciation. There was nothing he could do about it now, however; what was said was said and there was no way of reversing it. Besides, he had a new problem to think about now—he had no horse and he doubted Zeb Oliver had one he could use.

"He awake yet?" a man's deep voice asked in the adjoining room.

"Awake and hungry," Dixie replied. "You want anything?"

"Nope, leastwise not right now. I'll just go in and take a look at our pilgrim."

Zeb Oliver, somewhere in his sixties Rye guessed, was tall, lean and leathery-looking. He had a cropped beard, full mustache, and his eyes were dark and flint-sharp. Dressed in denim pants and jacket, he also wore a red and black checked wool shirt, a battered old Union army hat and well-scarred boots.

"Name's Zeb Oliver," he said, extending his hand. "Pleased to see you looking a bit more pert. Yesterday morning I wouldn't't've give you a copper for your chances of living after a tumble like you took."

"Seems I've got you and your niece to thank for keeping me alive."

"Yeh, reckon so. Me and the little gal happened to be right close when you and your horse come sliding and bouncing down the slope. Got you in and doctored up first off. Couldn't find nothing busted, which sure surprised me. You was bleeding right smart in a few places, however."

Rye looked at his bandaged arms and hands, and reaching up, gingerly touched the cloth encircling his head. There was soreness anyplace his fingers explored, and the movement brought a stab of pain to his shoulder.

"What the hell was you a'doing riding so close to the edge of the trail? I don't figure you for no greenhorn."

"Horse didn't slip."

"Then how—"

"Was shoved. I'd been tracking an outlaw. Followed him from town. Name's Hode Wilkinson. Lives up around here somewhere."

Zeb nodded slowly. "Should've guessed that seeing as

how you're a lawman." The older man's features had tightened.

The sound of meat sizzling in a frying pan and the good odor of freshly baked cornbread were drifting into the room through the open doorway to the kitchen.

"Expect Dixie's done told you about your horse. The critter busted his neck falling down the slope."

"Yes, she did," Rye said. Oliver's attitude had changed since he had learned the details of the fall from the trail, and that Hode Wilkinson was the cause of it. It was evident that Oliver feared the outlaw. "Need to get out of here and on his trail again. You know where I can get a horse?"

Oliver seemed relieved at Rye's words. "Yeh, maybe I do. Mind telling me what you're after Wilkinson for? Been told he's a mighty bad one, killings and such. Ain't never much said about him around here."

"He's wanted for murdering, for jailbreak, for just about every crime you can think of. He's already been tried and sentenced to hang. I've been ordered to bring him in alive so they can put a rope around his neck."

The sizzling of the meat in the kitchen had ceased and shortly Dixie came through the doorway with a large plate of fried venison, potatoes and hot cornbread. Placing it before Rye, she took up his empty cup.

"I'll get you some more coffee."

The lawman nodded, returned her smile. Setting the plate in his lap, he took up the knife and fork and began to eat. Zeb moved back and leaned against the wall, and Dixie, returning with Rye's filled coffee cup as well as one for Zeb, took a place beside her uncle.

"Sure nice to have company even if he is all bunged up," she said as she brushed a stray lock of dark hair into place.

Oliver shrugged. "Ain't so sure of it being nice when you figure who he was after—and who's looking for him probably right now."

Rye, enjoying the tender venison, the mealy, fried potatoes and hot cornbread, paused. "Been thinking about that myself. I'll move on soon as I get my clothes on. Sure don't aim to make trouble for you folks."

"You're not able to go anywhere," Dixie said with a frown. She turned to Zeb. "What's he mean—cause us trouble?"

"His horse didn't slip off the trail, was pushed off."

"Pushed off!" Dixie echoed. "Who would—"

"The marshal was chasing Hode Wilkinson."

"Know that—"

"Aims to take Hode in for hanging. Hode must've hid in the brush and when the marshal come by he jumped out and shoved his horse over the edge. Plenty of narrow places along the trail where he could've done it, and big and strong as Wilkinson is, it wouldn't be no chore for him."

Rye watched the woman's face as Zeb related the details of the incident. She had paled slightly, her soft, creamy skin now gray. The possibility of the outlaw coming there to the cabin looking for the man he'd pushed over the edge of the trail apparently frightened her.

"I'm obliged to you for a fine meal," the lawman said, finishing off the meat and potatoes and taking a swallow of the coffee. "If you'll just get me my clothes I'll be on my way."

"On foot?" Oliver said. "Mister lawman, you wouldn't get nowhere the shape you're in. Maybe if you had a horse to ride you'd make it a ways, but I misdoubt it."

"I'll manage," Rye said stubbornly. "They say Hode

lives around here somewhere. He has a horse, maybe a couple of them. I find him, I'll have a horse."

"You got any idea where his cabin is?"

"No. Was hoping you could help."

Zeb scratched at his beard. "It's somewhere on the far side of the ridge. Know that much but just exactly where I sure can't tell you." Oliver paused and then said, "Wilkinson is a jasper you don't get friendly with. He'd as soon cut your throat as say howdy."

Rye twisted about, threw his legs over the side of the bed. "My clothes. If you'll—"

Zeb stepped to the curtained closet built along the wall as Dixie gathered up the dishes and cups and hurried from the room. Pulling the drape aside, he took Rye's clothing from the nails serving as hooks and tossed them onto the bed.

"The little gal sort of fixed them up for you," he said. "We never get no company here except maybe a stray cowhand looking for the Hoffman Ranch, and she was hoping you'd stay a spell."

"I'm obliged to you and her but I've got to keep after Wilkinson. I'm not the only one on the mountain that is."

"You mean there's some more lawmen up here?"

"No, three Kiowa Indians. Wilkinson killed the father and mother of one and kidnapped his sister. He's got her with him—if she's not dead."

Rye got unsteadily to his feet, tried to ignore the pain in his shoulder and a similar throbbing in his leg.

"You ain't going nowheres, mister," Zeb said, wagging his head.

"Sure can't stay here!" the lawman shot back impatiently. "I'm not about to put you and your niece in danger from him."

"I appreciate that," Oliver said, "and I respect you for

it, but there ain't nothing you can do about it until I scare up a horse for you."

Rye, legs braced against the bed to remain standing, smiled tightly. "And while you're doing that there's a good chance those Kiowas will track down Wilkinson and take him back to their village—"

"Where they'll torture him for a spell and then kill him," Oliver finished. "Now, I can't see nothing wrong with that. Killing's killing and when a man's dead, he's dead."

Dixie returned from the kitchen, halting just inside the doorway, and leaned against the wall.

"Zeb, couldn't you cut across the mountains to the Hoffman Ranch and get the marshal a horse from them?" she suggested. "You could ride Old Blaze."

"Old Blaze?" Rye echoed.

Zeb nodded. "Old's right. Worn-out old workhorse we've got. More used to plowing than having somebody on his back. Wouldn't do you no good, but like the gal says I just might cross the mountains on him, was I to take it easy, and get to the Hoffman place."

Rye, hope lifting within him, unbuckled his money belt and removed three double eagles. Handing the gold coins to Zeb, he said, "Any chance you could leave right away?"

Oliver grinned. "You're a sudden sort of fellow, ain't you? Yeh, expect I can."

"Get me the best thing you can—I'll pay more if I have to. How long will it take?"

Zeb thrust the coins into a side pocket of his pants. "Well now, I ought to be back by evening tomorrow if everything goes right," he drawled. "Maybe a mite earlier."

Seven

HODE WILKINSON, hands still joined by Rye's connected steel cuffs now in front of instead of behind his back—a feat accomplished by sitting down and working the chain under his body and folded legs—watched the lawman and his horse tumble and bounce as they slammed into boulders and clumps of brush on their way down the precipitous slope.

That should finish the lawman, he thought. A hard smile parted his thick lips. He'd same as told the lawman earlier that he was wasting his time trying to arrest him and take him in to some two-bit jail. When were they going to learn that the law wasn't big enough to make a prisoner of him? He'd proved that to them time after time. They just seemed to never learn that it was best they leave him alone.

Cold, emotionless, he saw the big bay horse, his neck bent almost double, crash into a jutting finger of rock, saw the animal's flailing legs go limp. The horse was done for, that was sure. Wilkinson swore. That was a damn shame. He could have used a big, fine animal like the bay. The lawman—Rye he had said his name was—had reached the bottom, too. He lay crumpled against a bit of granite outcropping. Dead, too, no doubt. There was no point in climbing down to see.

Wilkinson reckoned the next best thing to do was return to his cabin and get rid of the chain cuffs. He had a sharp iron wedge and a double jack. The Indian girl could hold the wedge while he swung the hammer with one arm. She'd balk at doing it, but a couple of good bats to the side of her head would change her mind. That usually took any foolishness out of her and made her do what she was told.

Wilkinson's thoughts came to a halt. In the half light of early morning the old man and the girl who lived a short distance away up the valley had come into sight. They had heard the commotion set up by the horse and the lawman falling down the slope and had come out to see what it was all about.

He cursed again. He should have gotten rid of them years ago; now they'd be sticking their noses into his business by hauling the dead lawman in to town, or if the fall hadn't killed him, taking him in and doctoring him up. Either way he could expect the old man to go blabbing the story of what had happened all over the place, and word would eventually reach some lawdog and he'd have to start watching his back trail again for a spell.

But trouble of all kinds was no stranger to Hode Wilkinson. He'd been only a younker when his pa took him and his ma and headed west for the California goldfields. That they were getting in on the tail end of the rush didn't matter to his pa; they'd find enough to get by, or maybe even they'd hit it big, a man never knew. But such speculation counted for nothing. In Kansas they were jumped by an Indian war party. Both parents were killed, the wagon and its contents burned, and he, big for his size even then, was carried off by the Pawnees as a slave for one of the subchiefs.

He had managed to survive with the Pawnees for about ten years simply because he could do nothing else. During that time, however, he not only learned to know the Indians but became adept in their ways while all the time building a hatred for them for what they had done to him and his family.

One spring he had suffered all the abuse and cruelties he could take from the Pawnees, and on a dark night, had crawled into the tipi of the brave who had claimed him, murdered him and his squaw and made an escape. It would seem some kind of personal relief would have come from taking the lives of the two Indians who had beat and tortured him, but it had gone beyond that; he had developed a burning hatred not only for the Pawnee people who had degraded him but for all Indians regardless of tribe.

He fared no better with the whites. They considered him a renegade from the first encounter he had with a wagon train. Ignoring his plea for help voiced brokenly in the few words of English he remembered from childhood, they drove him off. They judged him by appearance, saw him as a huge, hulking red man dressed in deerskin pants, cotton shirt, moccasins, and fitted not only with a keen-bladed knife but a temper every bit as sharp.

Thus his feelings for whites quickly took its place on a level with his hatred for the Indians. He made no more attempts at being friendly with either, and influenced by the brutal existence he had led with the Pawnees, began a life based solely upon survival.

He stole whenever the opportunity presented itself, killed when necessary, while all the time growing larger in stature, and more cold-blooded by nature, fully aware of the legend that was gradually shrouding him. He robbed stagecoaches at will despite the presence of shotgun riders. Merchants in the smaller settlements fell prey to his depredation which occurred always at night when he came and went like a shadow.

Lawmen, never plentiful in the area around the Sangre de Cristo range, were increased. Posses roamed the slopes, the canyons and the flats of the great mountains to no avail. Wilkinson always eluded them.

He became known generally as One Ear since no one was actually aware of his real name or of his origin, and soon his existence was simply ignored. Men unconsciously assumed the credo that as long as they stayed clear of him, and were not the victim of his plundering, the wise thing to do was pretend he did not exist. This attitude in time had its effect on the local lawmen, and they, too, closed their eyes to the problem.

Wilkinson was smart enough to make the most of the situation, and carried on a life of lawlessness at will. He continued to rob, murder and rape at leisure, young Indian girls usually being the victims of his vicious attention. He built himself a cabin high in the Sangre de Cristos, so well concealed by the surrounding growth that it had yet to be detected by anyone. This was probably because no one was foolhardy enough to go looking for it.

Wilkinson, now squatting along the edge of the trail, spat angrily as he watched the old man and the girl pick up the limp body of the lawman and carry it to their cabin. He'd best keep an eye on the old man. It could be the lawdog was still alive. That meant but one thing—he'd have to pay them a visit and finish the job.

Wolf Killer hunkered over the small fire they had built and chewed thoughtfully on the bit of rabbit torn from the carcass suspended over the flames. The day had passed and they had found neither the lawman nor the evil One Ear who had stolen Morning Sky and killed his parents, Spotted Antelope and Singing Dove. The knowledge of failure was filling him with deep bitterness that lay like a heavy rock in his belly.

"As I foretold, they did not come this way," Little Horse said. There was the usual, all-knowing finality in his tone that always irritated Wolf Killer and Brown Bear.

Wolf Killer paused to lick the grease off his fingers. Darkness had overtaken them high in the mountains—a vast, rugged area of canyons, peaks and slopes that were unfamiliar to him. That, too, made him uncomfortable.

"That we do not know for certain," he said, contradicting Little Horse as a matter of principle.

"What you say is true," Brown Bear added. "We cannot say for sure."

"We may not be sure of anything except we are in strange country, it is night, and I am cold and hurting," Little Horse said stiffly.

"If I had a blanket I would give it to you," Brown Bear said, sarcasm larding his voice. "Is this the first time you have been cold and hurt?"

The older brave tossed the leg bone of the rabbit he had snared earlier into the fire and gave his fingers a thorough cleaning with his tongue. He carefully probed the pad of leaves Brown Bear had applied to the wound in his shoulder after searing it with a hot knife. The lawman's bullet hadn't done much damage, having missed the bone and tearing the flesh, but there was pain.

"It is not. That you know. It is only that we have chosen the wrong trail to follow," Little Horse said.

"There were many trails," Wolf Killer said with a shrug of his bare shoulders. Shadows played on his copper torso as the flames of the fire flickered, throwing their yellow glow into the night. "We chose the one upon which there were the most tracks. You do not think the choice was wise?"

"I think only that it was the wrong trail. I would have chosen the one to the north."

Wolf Killer listened momentarily to the distant wail of a coyote and then again shrugged. "A trail which no doubt would have led us out of the mountains. At the time we were all agreed that One Ear went up the trail, as did the lawman."

"Why do we talk of something that cannot be changed?" Brown Bear said impatiently, throwing aside his bit of rabbit. "When the sun comes up we should go back down the mountain and search for tracks."

Wolf Killer nodded. "That will be the wise thing to do. We must find the trail left by One Ear and see where he turned off. There will also be the tracks of the lawman."

"What of the cabin in the valley below the trail? Is it likely that is the home of One Ear?"

Wolf Killer shook his head. Now that the fire had dwindled to a glow, the night around him had become alive with sounds—the sleepy stirring of birds, the rustle of small animals in the dry leaves, the clicking of insects one of which, attracted by the faint light of the coals, fluttered past him and fell into the near-dead fire.

"No. We were told he has a secret place, one that cannot be found. The cabin is very much in the open for all to see."

"Who can believe a white man?" Little Horse protested. "They are the ones who say that. We should see for ourselves."

"It would waste time. The reasoning of a child tells you

that the cabin is well hidden, otherwise it would have been found by other lawmen long ago."

"Nevertheless I think it would be wise to see," Little Horse said stubbornly.

Wolf Killer took the last piece of rabbit from its place over the glowing coals. He glanced at Brown Bear. His friend who was to be his brother-in-law had curled up by the graying ashes and was apparently asleep.

"This we can settle when the sun appears," Wolf Killer said with a nod to Little Horse, and began to tear at the thin meat of the rabbit's carcass with his strong teeth. He would still be hungry when he was finished, he knew.

Eight

RYE AWOKE early that next morning. His shoulder and hip still ached sullenly, as did the remainder of his body, but with a lesser intensity. Ignoring the discomfort, he lay quiet, savoring the good smell of boiling coffee. Shortly Dixie appeared in the doorway looking bright and cheerful.

"You awake?" she asked, and then added, "I can see you are. I'll put some meat and eggs on the stove and we can have breakfast. How do you feel? Coffee's ready."

Rye grinned at the rapid barrage of words coming from the girl. "Like I'm alive and that's about all."

Dixie laughed. "You took quite a fall but it'll wear off after you get up and move around a bit. I can heat up some water so you can take a bath if you want—it might help some. Washtub's the biggest thing we've got, though. It barely holds me."

Rye smiled. "Expect that's a pretty sight."

Dixie blushed. "It's up to you," she said after a bit. "I can put a kettle of water on and—"

"Never mind. I'll pass it up . . . That coffee sure smells good."

Dixie immediately turned back to the kitchen. She reappeared moments later with a cup of the steaming brew in her hand. Outside, beyond the red elderberry brush that grew against the cabin and partly blocked the window, Rye could hear a bird singing. The partial view of the world available to him showed the valley lifted gently toward higher ground in the west, and beyond its horizon towered a brush- and tree-covered ridge with a brilliant blue sky backdrop.

Still holding the cup of coffee in both hands, Rye studied the young woman as she turned away. Her beauty was more apparent in the light of day now that he had time and ease to consider her. After thanking her departing figure, he began to sip the hot liquid. It was to his exact liking and he waited until he had finished off the cup before he started dressing.

By the time he was up and on his feet, a bit light-headed and unsteady, he could hear the sizzle of meat on the stove coming from the kitchen, and slowly made his way to that room. Each step was painful but John Rye was an old hand at surviving and weathering injury, and gave the pain little thought. He was alive and that's what counted; the pain would pass, and he would be himself again.

He'd leave just as soon as Zeb Oliver returned with a horse. His being there with the girl and the old trapper endangered them both if Hode Wilkinson was aware they had taken him in after the fall down the slope. And there was little doubt in the lawman's mind that he knew.

"It'll be ready in just a couple more minutes," Dixie said, glancing over her shoulder as he entered the room. "Get yourself some more coffee and sit down to the table."

Rye did as he was directed, watching the young woman go about her cooking chores with businesslike efficiency.

This was what it would be like to have a home, he thought, all the good smells of cooking, the quiet orderliness that a woman brought to a house, the set, day-by-day sameness that was also a part of it. Rye shook his head. Such was not for him, he told himself once again. He had one trail in life to follow, that of being a lawman, and he'd stick to it.

"Are you hungry?"

Rye became aware of Dixie's voice. He grinned, nodded. "Caught me woolgathering, I reckon . . . I sure am. The smell of that meat frying and those hot biscuits would bring a dead man out of his grave."

The marshal rose, pleased at the laugh his words had evoked from the young woman, and setting his empty cup on the table, walked to the open door. Caution was an ingrained part of John Rye, and it came to him as natural as breathing.

"You ever see Wilkinson around here?" he asked, keeping slightly back from the opening.

He put his attention to the north where the trail cut its way across the mountain's rocky slope. The outlaw had hidden in the scrubby growth on its inner side, had come charging out from it to force the bay to the edge of the trail. Big and strong as Wilkinson was, it was not hard for him to shove the horse over the side.

There was no one on the trail or anywhere else in that part of the valley as near as he could tell. Nevertheless Rye felt it would be wise to keep a close watch. Wilkinson just might have seen Zeb and Dixie carry him into the cabin. It was the second time the thought had occurred to him, and that in itself was a sort of premonition. He'd best keep himself ready.

"No," Dixie replied, as she wiped her hands on the dish towel she was holding, "only people we ever see are back-peddlers and trappers looking for a river big enough to set their traps in. Once we did have a man and his family traveling in a wagon. Said they were headed for Utah. This valley is pretty much off the beaten track."

Rye nodded. Such had both advantages and disadvantages. It was all to the good for a man wanted by the law and seeking to avoid people, but bad for one who became ill or injured and needed help. However, it was what Rye expected to hear. Hode Wilkinson, like the birds, was too smart to mess in his own nest. He'd never do anything to draw attention to the area where he lived.

"Everything's ready," Dixie said, turning back to the stove.

Rye returned to his side of the room and waited in silence while the young woman set a plate of venison, fried eggs and potatoes before him. To that she added a pan of hot biscuits and a small mason jar of jelly—raspberry he guessed, made from the bushes he'd noticed growing on the mountainside. Refilling his coffee cup and her own, Dixie moved toward her place at the opposite side of the table. Rye was behind her and pulled out her chair to seat her. At his show of politeness she looked up at him.

"Thank you," she said softly.

He inclined his head slightly and went back to his place at the table. "Want to say this is a mighty fine breakfast," he said, taking up his knife and fork and beginning to eat. "Man on the move like I am don't often get a meal like this."

Dixie, her eyes still glowing from the courtesy the lawman had shown her, smiled. "I like to cook, but with only Zeb and me, I don't get the chance very often to fix anything special."

They continued the meal in silence for several minutes and then Dixie sat back and faced Rye squarely.

"I've had this on my mind ever since we carried you in from that fall."

The lawman paused. Just outside the door, waiting for sweepings from the kitchen floor, were two camp-robber jays, their bright, hard eyes cocked expectantly.

"That right?"

"You came here to get Wilkinson. When you do where will you take him?"

"To the jail in Springtown. If it turns out it don't look like it'll hold him, I'll take him on to Cimarron—a bigger town on to the south."

"I've heard of it. Only place I've been since Zeb brought me here is Springtown."

Rye took a swallow of his coffee, shook his head. "Towns are all pretty much the same. Just different in size."

"I was about ten when my folks were killed and Zeb took me over. I didn't have any other relatives, leastwise that I knew of. Where do you go after you put Wilkinson in jail?"

"Wichita. It's a town in Kansas. Sort of make it my headquarters."

"Is it a big town?"

"Yeh, I reckon you could say it is."

Dixie sat perfectly still, hands folded in her lap. Eyes bright and hopeful, she leaned forward. "Take me with you, Marshal—please! I've just got to get away from here, from . . . from this nothing life!"

Rye frowned. The last thing he wanted once he had Hode Wilkinson in chains, not to mention the very real probability of trouble with the Kiowas, was to have a woman on his hands to look out for.

"I don't see how I can," he said, seeking a way to gently douse the hope in the girl's heart. That she was lonely and hungry for the company of others was understandable, but he didn't see how he could help.

"Aren't there other families around here—people your age?"

"Well, yes, at the Hoffman Ranch. That's where Zeb went after a horse for you. They're the closest."

"Ought to be some cowhands around there, some who—"

"There are," Dixie said, settling back in her chair and lowering her eyes. "There was one I got to know real good. His name was Ethan—Ethan Wells. We were going to get married one spring but he got killed the winter before. His horse fell on him."

"That was hard luck," Rye said. "Sorry to hear it. Just can't figure why things sometime happen like that, but you're young. There'll be another like this Ethan."

"Not for me. I just want to get out of here and start living some other way—not that I don't appreciate all Zeb's done for me—but there must be more to life than this."

Rye tipped his cup to his lips and drained it. "I reckon life's just what you make it—good or bad."

"I suppose, but it seems others have made my life for me," Dixie said dispiritedly. "Marshal, I'm asking again— begging you actually—take me with you. I won't be any trouble. I can ride good and I'll look after myself, and I've got about a hundred dollars saved up that came from selling my folks' belongings. I can buy my own horse, and I'll pay my way."

"What about Zeb?" Rye said, struggling to get away from the subject.

"He won't mind. I expect he'll be happy to get me off his hands. He'll be free to do what he wants."

The lawman stirred uneasily. "But where would you

go? What will you do? Your hundred dollars won't last forever."

"Maybe I could go to Wichita. You said it was a big town. I could find a job there."

"Doing what? There're not many jobs for women except in a saloon, and you don't want that."

"I hear that in some places it's a respectable job. That in the bigger saloons they have what they call calico girls. They don't have to do anything but wait on tables, not entertain the men like they do in the ordinary saloons. Or maybe I could get a job as a cook in a restaurant—or I could teach school. I've done a lot of reading. Hardly anything else to do around here. Or maybe—"

"Lot of maybe's," Rye said. "Sure don't like throwing cold water on your ideas, but it's a tough world out there, even for a man."

"Please just think about taking me, Marshal. Will you do that much?"

Rye shrugged. "Can do that much," he said, pushing back his chair. "First off, however, I've got to catch Hode Wilkinson. Not going anywhere till then. Want to thank you for a fine meal," he added, and, getting to his feet, returned to his room.

He wished Dixie Oliver hadn't made her request. Looking after Wilkinson would be a big enough task without having the young woman to worry about. He didn't doubt she thought she could take care of herself but she didn't really know what it would be like—especially if the Kiowas showed up and gave him trouble. He had promised to think about it but the words of a refusal were already taking shape in his mind.

Strapping on his gun, he stood in the center of the room and practiced his draw. He needed to work the stiffness and soreness out of his arm and shoulder before Zeb returned, for that was when he planned to head up onto the mountain and search out Wilkinson.

Several times he made fruitless trips to the back door of the cabin to study the trail and the slope beyond for signs of the outlaw and the Kiowas. To him the Indians posed as much danger as Wilkinson.

But such was all a part of the calling John Rye had chosen to follow. Problems were nothing new, and the odds always seemed to be stacked against him, this time a bit higher perhaps. Hode Wilkinson was unlike any outlaw he had encountered before—a huge, powerful man, cruel, crafty, devoid of fear and utterly without conscience.

He'd make out all right. He always had even when there'd been some distraction like the Kiowas with which to contend. The only thing he had to do was get back in shape, concentrating particularly on his arm and shoulder —and hope that Dixie would change her mind about wanting to leave with him.

Nine

AROUND NOON of the following day Zeb Oliver returned—several hours ahead of his prediction. He was riding a gray mare and leading a muscular-looking buckskin gelding that took Rye's approval at first glance.

"Had to pay forty dollars for him," the trapper said apologetically. "Was the best I could do. Hoffman had a bay he was willing to sell, too, but he was a mite cross-grained and some older than Hoffman claimed he was."

"Where's Old Blaze?" Dixie asked, rubbing the mare's neck.

"Well, Hoffman took a fancy to him right off. Said he'd been looking for a real gentle old horse for his little grandson. Wanted to trade."

"Trade?" Dixie echoed. "He's got dozens of horses!"

"Got a big bunch all right—thirty or forty at least in what he calls his *remuda*, but they're all mustangs, and a mite too wild for the boy. Said Old Blaze was just what he was looking for and offered to trade me the mare for ten dollars difference. Owe him that."

"You had ten dollars left over from buying the buckskin. Why didn't you pay him right then?" Rye wondered.

"Weren't my money, was yours."

"You could have gone ahead and used it. Would have been all right with me."

"Maybe so, but that ain't how I seen it. You wasn't there to tell me it'd be all right. Ain't no big deal, I'll scrape up the ten dollars and get it to him soon as I can."

Rye shrugged, and ran his hand along the buckskin's neck down to the shoulder. The horse remained quiet.

"Couldn't have done any better picking myself, Zeb," he said, glancing up the slope to the trail. There was no sign of anyone. "I'm much obliged to you. How about keeping that ten for your trouble?" he added as Oliver held out the eagle change Rye had coming.

"Weren't no trouble," the trapper said, "and I sure don't take no pay for doing a man a favor."

"Was a business deal, not a favor."

"Ain't the way I see it," Oliver replied and turned to the horses. Dixie was still making friends with the mare. "I'll put them both in the shed till you're ready to pull stakes, Mister Doomsday Marshal," he said with a grin. "Heard all about you over at Hoffman's."

A wry smile pulled at the lawman's mouth. He'd never be able to get away from the name they'd hung on him, he thought, and cut back to the house. He'd like to look the buckskin over a bit more, perhaps ride him for a bit to get acquainted, but he was reluctant to be seen in the open around Oliver's cabin.

Dixie was at his heels when he reached the doorway. Her eyes were filled with curiosity. "What did Zeb say they called you at Hoffman's? Some kind of a marshal."

"Been called a lot of things, none of which I'd want you to hear," Rye said and passed on into the cabin.

He started to look around for a place to hide the ten-dollar gold piece he felt Zeb had more than earned, and then gave up the idea. Men like Oliver had certain definite ideas about such things; it would be an insult to the old trapper as well as to Dixie when they found it. He'd try to think of some other way to repay them.

Standing at the window and looking off into the grassy valley, he wondered what Dixie would think of him when she learned he was known as a killer marshal. Would she understand that at times it was necessary to use his gun to carry out his duties? What would she think when told he had slain three men only a couple of days earlier in the saloon at the foot of the mountain?

Rye paused as he examined the contents of his saddle-bags—extra shirt, pants, socks, underwear, two boxes of .45 bullets, the short-barreled pistol that he kept in re-serve. Why was he troubling himself about Dixie and what she might think of him? Certainly a man needed the respect of others, both men and women, but he had to keep in mind that his sworn duty came first, and if such earned him the disrespect of others it was simply his bad luck.

"Seems you're a mite pearter," Oliver said from the doorway. "Nothing special go on while I was away?"

"Nope," Rye answered, turning about. "Kept an eye on the trail thinking maybe Wilkinson or the Kiowas might show themselves."

"Critters like them do their doings at night, in the dark," Zeb said, and pointed at Rye's gear. "You fixing to leave?"

"Figured I'd wait till morning—if it's jake with you."

"Jake with me and with Dixie, too, I expect. She was asking all about you—just what I'd heard at Hoffman's and such."

"Sorry you had to tell her," the lawman said with a shrug. He was wondering at the moment if Dixie had said anything to Zeb about her leaving. "Word gets around that's not always true."

"It's true they call you the Doomsday Marshal, ain't it?"

Rye nodded. "Can't say that I'm particularly proud of it."

"And the talk is that you're the gol-dangdest lawman that ever wore a badge—that you always get the man you're chasing, even the worst kind."

"Talk like that gets stretched a bit as time goes on."

"Maybe. Hoffman said you was a special kind of badge-toter, that they unload the job of catching the worst kind of outlaw on you. Said he'd heard the governor had asked special for you to come and put the irons on Hode Wilkinson 'cause nobody else had ever been able to do it."

Rye swore wryly. "You and Hoffman must have done a helluva lot of talking!"

"I was listening mostly, and when all the jabbering was done, I felt mighty proud to have you under my roof."

"Just hope me being here won't cause you and Dixie any trouble from Wilkinson. I kept out of sight in case he was keeping an eye on the place."

"He couldn't've seen you from the trail when you was looking at the buckskin. Maybe earlier. Sure can't say for sure about that."

"I was careful," Rye said. "You think anybody at Hoffman's might know where Wilkinson's cabin is?"

"Figured you'd be asking that. Truth is, hardly ain't anybody done any looking for it. Expect they'd just as soon not even know him."

Zeb paused to glance toward the adjoining room where

a rattling of pans told him that Dixie was getting the next meal together.

"Was one fellow, howsomever, that claimed he'd been up there where they figure he's living. Little canyon off the north ridge."

"He give you any more directions than that?"

"Nope. Tried pinning him down and right then he sort of lost his memory, but I think I know about where it is he's talking about."

Rye came to attention. He leaned forward. Oliver scrubbed at his beard.

"Now, I ain't saying I can ride up there and point to the front door of his place, but I've been around here a lot of years and know just about every hoot and holler on the mountain."

Rye considered that thoughtfully. "Were you here before Wilkinson?"

"Far as I know. Never heard of him except in the last five maybe six years. Ain't saying he wasn't here afore that. If you're wanting, I reckon I can take you up to about where that cowboy seemed to think Wilkinson might have a cabin."

Rye, squatting on his haunches, unbuckled the other saddlebag pouch and began to probe about in it. More clothing, a few loose shotgun shells, a bottle of whiskey, a packet of wanted posters and some loose papers. He heaved a deep sigh.

"Sure relieves me to hear you say that. Will save me a lot of time, but I don't want you to get yourself crossways with Wilkinson," he said as he got to his feet.

"Reckon I can look after myself—and the little gal," Zeb said. "That cowhand claimed he'd seen a Indian girl up there, too. Said she was half naked and had a rope tied around her middle and then to a tree."

"Wilkinson kidnapped a girl—name is Morning Sky. It could be her."

"Yeh, expect so. I recollect you mentioning her. When do you want to start out? We ought to be on the trail way early, before sunup. That way we can get moving while it's still sort of dark."

"Suit me fine."

Zeb folded his arms, leaned back against the wall. "Expect that'll be about four o'clock by that ticker you're carrying. I'll have the little gal fix us up some grub, enough for a couple of days. If we ain't found his place by then we might as well quit looking. He'll be somewheres else."

"Pretty sure he's living right around here somewhere," Rye said. "Tracked him up the trail. He was headed for the top of the mountain."

"Yeh, expect he was."

Rye studied the older man from a side glance. It was not his practice to involve an outsider in any job assigned him, but with the Kiowas also searching for the big outlaw there was no time to be lost.

"Like to make it plain now, once we locate Wilkinson's cabin your part's over. I'll do the rest. Don't want you getting yourself shot up."

"Ain't the way I see it," Zeb said, shaking his head. "A man spots a rattlesnake a'sidling up to a bunch of folks not paying no mind, he don't turn around and go the other way—not if he's worth his salt, he don't. He kills that there rattler."

"I appreciate your wanting to help, but it's a matter for the law and I don't want you hurt."

"Ain't much chance of that. I've been living for sixty years more or less and I ain't never got hurt. Now, don't you worry none about old Zeb, you just be ready to ride about four o'clock in the morning."

"I'll be ready—friend," the lawman said and as Zeb turned and left the room, resumed checking the contents of his saddlebags.

Ten

"DONE MY FIGHTING with the Colorado Volunteers," Zeb said, striking a match and holding it to the charred bowl of the pipe clenched between his teeth. "You in the war?"

It was well after dark. The evening meal Dixie had prepared—biscuits, roast venison, baked potatoes flared with grease, boiled cabbage, wild onions, berry pie and coffee —was over and both Rye and the old trapper were enjoying a smoke as they sat at the kitchen table. Dixie was in her room on the other side of the cabin busy at some womanly chore.

The marshal nodded as he took the stogie from his mouth. "Was with Jenkin's Tennessee Cavalry until he was killed."

"That end it for you, too?"

Rye shook his head at the once rife rumor that in the Confederate army, when a company or regimental commander was killed, the rank-and-file soldiers under him threw down their arms and went home. The untrue canard no longer angered him.

"No, General McCausland took over. I rode with him after that."

"McCausland," Zeb murmured, blowing out a puff of smoke. "Ain't he the one that burnt down a whole town? Name was Chambersburg, I recollect."

"He's the one," Rye said and let the subject drop. He had engaged in too many arguments concerning the incident and didn't intend to get into one with Zeb Oliver now.

The older man settled back in his chair, blew another small cloud of smoke into the warm air. Earlier he had built a fire in the rock fireplace to take the chill off the room, as he put it, and the flickering light from the restless flames blended with that from the lamp on the table.

"Well, a lot of things happen in a war that don't make no sense," he said. "Some folks claimed McCausland was right, was only paying back the Union for what one of their generals had done to some rebs—tit for tat, you might say."

"Yes, I reckon you might say it that way."

"But I sure don't know. Burning down a whole town, a lot of it the property of folks who weren't even in the war —I ain't for certain—"

"When there's a war everybody's in it whether they want to be or not," Rye said indifferently. He wished Oliver would get off the subject. For some reason he was not at ease. Perhaps it was the conversation, or a premonition of things to come—he wasn't sure which.

"Yeh, and both sides figures they're in the right. I reckon you can't blame a fellow like McCausland. He thought he was doing right, even if he wasn't."

Rye stirred nervously. General Jubal Early, McCausland's superior, was the man responsible for the burning of the Pennsylvania town; he gave the order, McCausland simply carried it out.

"When you're in the army and you're given an order," he began, "you—"

Abruptly the door burst open. Rye lunged to his feet, hand instinctively going down to the .45 on his hip. Hode Wilkinson's huge, threatening shape filled the opening.

"What the hell—" Zeb Oliver started to say, and then his voice was drowned out by the blast of the rifle held by the outlaw.

Rye fired as Wilkinson surged into the room. Smoke from both weapons boiled up, began to fill the air. Rye was aware of Zeb Oliver's sliding off to one side and falling to the floor, overturning the table and sending the lamp crashing to the plank surface.

Rye's bullet hit the mountain man somewhere in the upper part of his body. The lead slug had little effect. Rye fired again as Wilkinson came on, triggering his rifle like a sixgun in his right hand, a long-bladed knife in the other.

"The law ain't getting me!" he thundered into the smoke-filled room.

Rye, circling the upset table, and hunched low, strained to see through the dense cloud. Fire had broken out on the floor where the lamp had fallen and was adding to the confused light.

"Zeb!"

Dixie's anguished cry reached the lawman. He saw the vague shape of the girl as she ran into the room and dropped to the side of her uncle. Wilkinson, still on the move, stumbled over Oliver's sprawled legs. He swore loudly, continued his uncertain circling in the pall, hoping for a shot at Rye.

Dixie drew away from Oliver's motionless body and got to her feet. She was little more than a crouched outline in the heavy smoke and weak light. Rye saw her pull a small hooked rug from the floor onto the steadily strengthening fire started by the spilled lamp, to smother it. The flames died instantly, further darkening the room but adding more smoke. Rye dropped back beside the young woman, caught her by the arm.

"Get out of here!" he yelled as Wilkinson again fired his rifle. "Hide somewhere!" He pushed her toward the outside door. "It's Wilkinson!"

He didn't know if Dixie had heard or not. In that same moment he collided with the outlaw as he, still bent low, turned about. The impact sent him to one knee. Wilkinson was upon him in only seconds. Rye saw the faint glitter of firelight on the knife Wilkinson held, saw it sweep down searching for him. The lawman threw himself to one side, rolled away and came to his feet. He saw the towering bulk of Wilkinson lunging for him. He triggered his .45. The outlaw hesitated as the bullet went into his body.

Rye, taking advantage of the moment, got his feet squarely under himself, wondering all the while if Dixie was all right, if she had escaped the choking smoke and reached safety outside the cabin. A curse ripped from his lips as he saw her. She was a dim shape lying crumpled in a corner of the room. Either she had been hit by one of Wilkinson's bullets, or the outlaw had struck her with his knotted fist, knocking her to the floor.

"You, lawman!" Wilkinson's voice was harsh and loud. "You're done! I aim to blow your damned head clean off!"

The flames in the fireplace had all but died for lack of fuel. In the half dark Rye could barely see the huge shape of the outlaw. He was only a gray blur again circling the overturned table and knocked-aside chairs.

"Give it up, Hode!" Rye called back. "You're already shot up and I won't let you get out of here alive!"

"The hell with you!" Wilkinson shouted, and fired in the direction of Rye's voice.

The bullet tore through the lawman's shirt, burned across his rib cage. He staggered back, tripped over some of the debris littering the floor and went down.

Wilkinson yelled and rushed forward. "You ain't getting out of here alive!"

The marshal saw the hulking shape move in. He raised his .45 and squeezed the trigger. It was too late to take aim or shoot for any particular area. It was down now to a matter of kill or be killed.

Wilkinson cursed, halted as he clutched his arm. Rye instantly kicked free of the entangling chair and came to his feet, eyes searching for the outlaw. The weak moonlight coming through the doorway ended suddenly. Rye wheeled, gun up and ready. Wilkinson's shape filled the doorway.

"Hold right there!" Rye shouted.

But the outlaw staggered on. Rye aimed low for one of the big man's legs. He would stop him that way rather than kill him, thereby fulfilling the order he had been given. He pressed the trigger. The gun's hammer clicked metallically. The cartridge was either spent or dead.

Grim, the lawman hastily thumbed a fresh shell from his belt and crossed the room in three long strides. After rodding out an empty cartridge, he pushed a fresh load into the .45's cylinder. He halted at the doorway.

The quick beat of a horse leaving fast reached him. Rye swore deeply. Hode Wilkinson had escaped him again.

Eleven

RYE TURNED, hurriedly crossed the dark room to where Dixie lay. She was sitting up dazedly rubbing the side of her head. The lawman, a strong flow of relief coursing through him, moved to the fireplace, threw wood onto the graying coals and fanned the fresh fuel into flames. The girl was apparently all right; evidently she had been struck by the outlaw and knocked, semiconscious, into the wall. As light again began to fill the still smoke-filled room, he turned to Oliver. He knelt and felt for a pulse.

"He's—he's dead, isn't he?" Dixie said. It was more a statement of fact than a question. Even before Rye could answer, she began to sob quietly.

"Afraid he is," the lawman said, coming to his feet. "Can chalk up another killing to Hode Wilkinson." He completed the reloading of his pistol. "Feel responsible for this. If I hadn't come here, it wouldn't have happened."

Dixie shook her head. "You can't blame yourself," she said, and went into an adjoining room to fetch another lamp. Rye, holstering his gun, righted the table and chairs, after which the young woman set the lamp in place and lit it with a brand from the fire.

"You can look at it in another way," she said as she stepped back. "If Wilkinson hadn't pushed you and your horse off the trail you wouldn't have been here in the first place."

Rye made no comment but he supposed her oblique reasoning had some truth to it. Crouching beside Oliver's stiffening body, he took up the dead man, followed Dixie into the small bedroom where the old trapper had slept, and laid him on his bunk.

"I'll see if I can find some planks and nail a coffin together," he said.

"No need," Dixie replied. "There's one out in the shed that Zeb made. Said he thought it best to have one ready."

"You want me to get it?"

"Whatever you like." The young woman's voice was listless and broken, and continual weeping had turned her eyes red. "It can wait for morning. First I have to wrap him in the patch quilt Mary made for him. Told me he wanted to be buried in it when his time came."

"Mary? Was that his wife?"

"No, Zeb never married," Dixie said, taking the quilt off a shelf in a curtained closet. "I don't know exactly who she was, but she was good to him—and good to me —like a mother. Zeb explained it all to me when she left."

"I don't need to know this—"

"I'd like for you to hear it," Dixie said while she spread the patchwork quilt. "She was married to a man and lived in a cabin somewhere the other side of Brimtown. He threw her out when she got mixed up with a peddler who had stopped by one day. She just showed up here at Zeb's, sick and almost dead from hunger and the weather, he said, and he took her in.

"That was five or six years before I came to live with him. I liked her a lot. She taught me how to cook and sew and keep house. She was responsible for fixing this place up—for the chickens and the garden and things like that. We got along fine, same as she and Zeb did. Then one day she just disappeared without a word."

"You or Zeb ever hear from her again?"

"Never did. Zeb had given her some gold—a little canvas bag of nuggets he'd found somewhere in a stream up on the mountain—"

"Gold—around here?"

"Zeb thought it had washed down from some higher place during a big storm. I think he spent some time looking for it but without any luck. Always warned me to not talk about it to anyone. Said it would start a gold rush in this part of the country, and ruin it."

Dixie paused. She had wrapped the quilt about the body of Zeb Oliver, and was now fastening the edges together with needle and coarse thread.

"I miss Mary—missed her terribly at first. I guess I still do. We used to talk for hours, and we read a lot, newspapers, magazines, books, anything Zeb could find in town to bring home. And of course we had the Bible. I—I owe her a lot. She furnished the schooling that I didn't get."

Dixie had finished linking the edges of the patch quilt together, and stepping back, laid the needle and thread aside. She turned to Rye.

"If you don't mind I'd like to be alone with him for a spell."

"Sure," Rye said. "I'll go find that coffin and get a grave ready. Anyplace special you think he'd like to be buried?"

"There's a little hill just below here. Already has a grave on it—I don't know whose. When I asked Zeb one day he didn't answer me. I think that's where he'd like to be."

The lawman turned without comment, pausing long enough as he passed through the adjoining room to throw more wood into the fireplace. Then he lit the lantern he found hanging outside the doorway and made his way across the yard, past the spring and to the shed where the coffin was said to be.

It was standing on one end in a back corner, well covered with dust. Locating a spade, and leaving the pine box where it was, Rye went to the hill Dixie had indicated and spent the next two hours hollowing out a grave in the soft, dark loam.

Earlier he had hoped to be on his way after Wilkinson with Zeb as his guide, but that was all changed. He now had more reason than ever to capture the killer, and this time he'd not let the outlaw get away. This time he would kill him, despite his orders, rather than let him escape.

He could forget about getting an early start. It was necessary that he help Dixie with the burial, and keep her company until she had regained her composure. Likely a couple or three more hours would make little difference. Wilkinson had been shot twice, possibly three times, Rye was sure. Just how bad it was hard to say but for certain he'd not go far. It was a good bet that he'd head for his cabin, which, according to what information he'd been able to get, was somewhere near the ridge crowning the nearby slope.

The grave dug, Rye dropped back to the shed and dragged the coffin out to where he could ready it. Finding a hammer, he removed the partly fastened-down lid and inspected the box's interior. It was unlined but the cracks between the boards had all been sealed with pitch. Taking it, the hammer and a few extra nails, the lawman returned to the grave, then doubled back to the cabin. Dixie was standing beside the quilt-wrapped body of Oliver. She half turned to face him.

"He wanted to live to be a hundred," she murmured. There was a faint tremor in her voice.

"That would be a long time in this world," Rye said. "Not sure I'd want that."

"Neither would I," Dixie replied. Then, "Do you believe in heaven, Marshal?"

Rye shrugged. "I reckon every man does—specially if he's been through hell."

Dixie considered that for a long moment. "I expect that's right. Is everything ready?"

He nodded, and stepping up to the bed, took up the body of Zeb Oliver and started for the door. Dixie took a shawl from a peg in the wall, fell in behind him and together they walked to the grave. After laying the dead man in the coffin, Rye put the lid in place and nailed it down securely. He slid the coffin into the open grave and stepped back. He picked up the hammer and returned to the shed leaving Dixie alone with the man who had taken her in and raised her when she was orphaned.

When he glanced toward the gravesite a short time later, Dixie was walking slowly back to the cabin. Rye crossed immediately to the grave, and taking up the spade, covered the coffin and mounded it properly. There was no marker; he would remember to make one before he left.

Dixie was cramming clothing into a flour sack when he entered the cabin to get his gear. Another sack containing food was on the table along with a frying pan, a small kettle, cups, a coffeepot and two each of forks, knives and spoons.

"We won't need those things if you already have them," she said, pointing at the utensils. She had dressed, was again in pants, checked wool shirt, short boots and misshapen hat.

Rye stopped short. He had considered the fact that the

girl would now be alone in the cabin and probably unsafe but had not given it any further thought. His mind was occupied with other pressing needs.

"Where will you be going?" he asked.

The first pale streaks of dawn were showing along the eastern horizon and in the wire pen near the shed a rooster crowed.

"With you," Dixie replied. "I can't—won't stay here alone." She paused, glanced about. "I've never been afraid in my life, but now, after that outlaw—after he broke in and killed Zeb—I—"

Rye shook his head. "I'll be hunting him. I won't be able to—"

"What else can I do?" Dixie demanded. Her eyes were swollen from weeping and her features were haggard.

"Couldn't you go over to the Hoffman Ranch?"

"Not alone. It's a long ride, and with Wilkinson on the loose—"

"Sure don't see how you can come with me," Rye said. "I'll be on the move all the time, and when I catch up with him there's bound to be shooting. You could get hurt, maybe killed."

"I'll look out for myself. I can ride, and I'll be on a good horse. And I can shoot. Zeb has a shotgun that I used to hunt rabbits and sage hens. Just don't worry about me— I'll not get in your way. And you can leave me at the first town we come to when you start back with that outlaw."

"It may take days running him down—"

"I thought of that, too," Dixie said immediately. "I've put extra grub in that sack—enough to last several days. And we can kill rabbits and squirrels for fresh meat. Besides I can help you. I know about where Wilkinson's cabin is."

Rye frowned, gently rubbed that place where Wilkinson's bullet had seared his skin. "Have you been up there?"

"No, but I heard Zeb talking about it. I could find it without any trouble . . . There's blood on your shirt. Were you hit by one of that outlaw's bullets? Everything's happened so fast I forgot to ask if you were hurt."

"Bullet burned across my ribs," he said, shaking off the question. "No harm done."

Dixie had it all worked out, that was evident. And while the lawman disliked the thought of having her along, he could see that he had no choice.

"You can't stay here, that's for sure," Rye said after a time, "and I owe Zeb and you a big favor. Have I got your word that you'll do exactly what I tell you?"

"I promise," Dixie said quickly.

"Aim to hold you to that promise," Rye said, and taking up his gear, turned to the door. "I'll go saddle the horses. In another hour it'll be light enough to ride out."

Twelve

ALTHOUGH THE SUN had not as yet made its appearance in the east, it was light when Rye and Dixie rode away from the cabin. Rye found the buckskin Zeb had bought for him willing and easy to handle, responding to his every command. Dixie's horse, the gray mare that her uncle had made a trade for, also showed that she had been well trained and could be depended upon to do all that was expected of her.

As they moved away from the shed, Rye, cautious as always, made a careful study of the country around them as well as of the trail above. It was logical to believe that Hode Wilkinson would strike for his cabin, being wounded, but Wilkinson was no ordinary man; his injuries could be minor to him while severe to one of usual strength. Too, there were the Kiowas to think of. It would be sheer folly to ignore the possibility of their presence simply because there had been no sign of them. There were no riders to be seen in any direction. The lawman turned to Dixie, riding on his left.

"Is there a place along here where we can climb up to the trail?"

"About a mile farther on," Dixie replied.

She had said nothing since they had loaded up and she had gone to Zeb Oliver's grave for a final farewell, a matter of ten minutes or so. She had returned, eyes shining, and climbed upon the mare. Evidently she'd had a few bad moments at the grave, and respecting her feelings John Rye had said nothing, but he did note that as they rode away from the cabin she had kept her attention straight ahead, never looking back even once at the place that had been her home for many years.

The morning in the high valleys of the mountains was cool and clear. Clouds floated majestically above the rugged peaks and ridges, and the trees marching up the slopes like soldiers in rank were a dark green. Overhead the sky was a gray-blue that would gradually change to a more brilliant and clear color as the day lengthened and the land warmed under the sun's rays.

John Rye, a man of stern reality, viewed it all with a sort of wistfulness. Growing up on the Tillico Plains country of Tennessee, he had a natural affection for the land, but the profession he had chosen as his life's work never permitted him to remain long in one place. That, however, did not prevent his appreciating the areas he had occasion to pass through while carrying out his duties as a lawman.

Off to his right among the pines, he saw movement. The ever present possibility of Hode Wilkinson or the Kiowa braves being somewhere close by brought him up sharp. But it was only a buck mule deer and his harem of five does moving slowly through the lesser trees and brush.

"Here's where we can get up to the trail."

Dixie's voice sounded normal. She was his responsibility now, Rye reminded himself. What was once a disturbing, unwelcome thought was now a reality. He swore silently. Always a loner, he resented being burdened with a companion, particularly when the companion was a woman. It was not that he held anything personal against women; he enjoyed their company at the right time and in the proper setting. To John Rye it was simply a matter of priorities; the job and carrying it to a successful conclusion always came first.

They had turned into the cleft in the slope and were nearing the trail. Rye shifted on his saddle.

"You made any plans?"

Dixie shook her head. "No, not anything special other than what I talked to you about. Everything just sort of happened so fast that I . . ." Her voice trailed off into nothingness.

"Did at that," Rye agreed.

Raising himself in the stirrups, the lawman gave the slope and the approach to the trail swift scrutiny. He saw nothing but the scrubby growth and scattering of rocks that characterized the lower areas.

"I'll try not to be any trouble to you," Dixie said.

"Just don't want to see you get hurt," Rye said, settling back. "Don't recall asking but don't you have any folks somewhere?"

Dixie shook her head. In the steadily strengthening sunlight her hair, uncovered at the moment, was a glossy black with a tinge of red showing through.

"Zeb said my mother's folks lived somewhere in the northeast. He was the only relative left on my father's side."

Rye, his eyes on a hawk soaring low over the valley, shrugged. "Looks like we'll have to get you to your mother's people."

"I don't even know their name or where they live. They didn't approve of Papa, and wouldn't have anything to do with my mother or him after they married."

"We'll have to find a way to get in touch with them."

"I wouldn't know how. Zeb never talked about them."

The cleft in the slope narrowed into a ragged path leading upward. Rye slowed the buckskin, allowed Dixie and the mare to pass by and start the final ascent, steep but with a solid footing of partly buried rocks and gravel. When they had reached the summit and were on the trail, Dixie turned to him.

"Anyplace special you want to start?"

"Zeb talked about a ridge. Seemed to think Wilkinson's cabin was somewhere in that area."

"That would be on west of here—and high up. I've hunted that part of the mountain a bit. Never saw anybody or any cabin."

"Zeb figured the cabin would be north of the ridge. Expect I'd best start looking there." The lawman paused, studied the slope rising before them. From that moment on, he thought, he'd best double his vigilance. Wilkinson and the Kiowas could be anywhere in the thickly forested country ahead. "If you like you could wait here."

Dixie was shaking her head before he had finished. "No, I'll stay with you! I—I keep seeing that giant—that huge animal back there in our cabin—his face and his eyes, both filled with hate. And the way he just threw you around and knocked things over—it was terrible!"

Rye grinned tightly. He had worked off most of the soreness and stiffness from the fall down the slope but the physical results of his encounter with Hode Wilkinson were still with him.

"Strong as a bull, I'll give him that," the lawman murmured.

"Are you going to use your gun on him this time, shoot him, I mean . . . kill him?"

"Only if I have to. Orders are to bring him in alive to be hung."

"Whoever gave you that order never knew Wilkinson," Dixie said, shaking her shoulders. "Certainly they've never seen him."

Rye smiled. "I'm used to it. This isn't the first time I've come against the likes of Wilkinson—maybe not as big but just as tough and mean in some other way. It never makes any difference—a gun equalizes things." The lawman paused, again searched the country about them with half-closed eyes. "We'd best ride the shoulder of the trail. Not likely to be spotted if we're not in the open."

They rode on, climbing steadily. They passed the point where Wilkinson had hidden and then appeared suddenly to force Rye's horse over the edge of the slope. A short distance farther on they drew abreast of Zeb's cabin, well below. The oblong of logs and earth-covered roof with its adjacent structures all looked small, like miniatures.

"We best turn off here to get to the ridge," Dixie said a short time later.

They swung off the trail onto a smaller path that began to make its way through the trees and brush. It was cool and shadowy and again Rye sharpened his alertness; it would be ideal country for an ambush—either by Wilkinson or the Kiowas.

The Kiowas . . . Brown Bear, Wolf Killer and Little Horse. Rye was certain now they had taken a wrong trail that first day just as he was equally certain they had realized their mistake and were now somewhere in the vicinity. That they could have encountered the outlaw and had him in their possession was a possibility, too, but somehow Rye felt that wasn't the case.

They topped out a slight rise and halted on its rocky backbone. The country around them had changed. Pines were less plentiful, their place having been taken by spruce, fir and more aspen. The low growth had altered, also. Mountain sorrel covered the ledges and in the swales rose-colored dwarf clover and patches of purple primrose. Off to Rye's left a grassy slope flowed into a small valley. Water sparkled in a twisting, narrow ribbon along its floor.

"Which way do you want to go now?" Dixie asked. "This is the lower end of the ridge. It runs on west for a couple of miles, I think, then sort of drops off into a canyon. I was there once with Zeb when—"

Rye raised his hand, drew up abruptly in the saddle. Half turning, he looked to the west, his craggy features a study in concentration.

"Smoke," he said softly. "Coming from that direction." He pointed to a dense stand of trees a bit north of them.

"Smoke?" Dixie faced the direction to which he had turned. She smiled, eyes brightening. "I smell it now! You think it's Wilkinson?"

"Him or the Indians," Rye said, studying the area. The smoke, a thin, wavering line barely visible, seemed to be coming from a cluster of trees that fanned out from the reddish surface of a cliff. "If it's Wilkinson he was a lot easier to find than I expected."

"I heard Zeb say several times that the men who came up here hunting him didn't want to find him."

"Could be," the lawman said. "Now stay close behind me."

Touching the buckskin with his spurs, he moved off the ridge and slanted for the thick stand of trees. As they drew nearer, the smell grew stronger.

They reached the edge of the cluster of spruce and fir trees. The red cliff was now directly to the left. Rye halted, weighing the question of whether to move along the base of the vertical formation or head directly into the closely bunched trees and brush.

He decided on the latter course, and nodding to Dixie, moved on. The growth became even more dense, slowing their progress while the odor of smoke became more pronounced. Rye pulled up short. Dixie crowded up beside him.

"What is it?" she asked in a tense whisper.

The marshal pointed ahead. "The cabin," he replied in a like tone. "Looks like we've found Hode Wilkinson."

Thirteen

THE CABIN was built in a small clearing fronting a cut in the cliff. Spruce and fir trees formed a screen, masking it from a casual glance, which made it all but impossible to notice. Off to one side of the sturdy-looking structure was a lean-to shed. Six horses stood in the shelter.

"The big white one," Rye said, pointing at the dozing animals. "That's the horse Wilkinson was riding when I saw him in Brimtown. Means he's inside." Turning, the lawman gave the young woman a direct look. "I want you to stay back here in the trees out of sight."

Dixie nodded. "You aim to just walk up there, open the door and go in?"

"You think of any other way?" Rye answered, and headed the buckskin for the windowless, blind side of the cabin.

Moving quietly through the trees Rye reached the squat, log structure and drew the buckskin to a halt. Dismounting, he stood for a few moments listening. Hearing no sounds that would indicate that he had been seen, the lawman drew his .45 and started along the rough log wall of the cabin toward its entrance. At the corner of the building he again stopped.

Back in the trees he could hear a rapid tapping as a woodpecker drilled hopefully away at a tree trunk in search of insects. High overhead several vultures soared in slow, graceful circles in the brilliant blue sky, and over in the crude lean-to one of the horses stamped wearily. All but the white had likely belonged to victims of the outlaw, murdered by him as they made their way along the trail. Wilkinson had simply taken possession of them after the pilgrims had been dispatched, and no doubt planned to sell them once things had quieted down.

Rye glanced toward the trees to the east. Dixie Oliver and the mare she was riding were barely visible in the shadows. He'd make some changes once he had Wilkinson in hand and was ready to start back. He'd relieve the mare of all the baggage the girl had brought along and make a pack animal out of one of these horses. This would enable them to make better time. A hard grin pulled at the lawman's lips. If he took Wilkinson in hand, he thought wryly. So far he'd been unable to accomplish the feat.

The day had warmed, and pulling off his vest, Rye stood for a brief time moving his arms about and flexing his muscles. He was still a bit stiff and his left shoulder, not yet fully healed from the fall down the slope, still pained some. The brawl in Zeb Oliver's cabin had aggravated it considerably but fortunately it didn't hinder the use of his gun.

He saw Dixie lift her hand in a small gesture, and nodding, continued on toward the door. Again the question *what has happened to the vengeance-bent Kiowa braves?* entered his mind. It seemed strange to him that he had seen no sign of them anywhere. Could they have been watching him, allowing him to track down Hode Wilkinson, and when the man was safely in custody plan an ambush somewhere along the trail back to Springtown or perhaps Cimarron? Rye swore at the thought. The Kiowas might try but that would be as far as they would get.

The marshal reached the edge of the doorway, ducking low as he passed under the small port left in the front wall for visibility. Motionless, gun in hand, Rye listened. He could hear scuffling as well as weeping. Wilkinson had evidently struck someone, probably the Indian girl, for one reason or another.

The best thing for humanity would be to let the Kiowas have Hode Wilkinson. The big, brutal mountain man would then get what was coming to him, but Rye's orders prevented that. The court wanted to make a public execution of the burly outlaw by hanging him, and it was his job to see that such took place.

Again glancing about to be certain there was no one else around but Dixie Oliver, Rye stepped up to the door. Gun cocked and ready, he drew back his leg, took a deep breath and kicked the slab wood panel inward.

A blast of stale, foul air all but rocked him back on his heels. Wilkinson cursed loudly as surprise hit him. In the poor light filtering in through a window high in the rear wall, the lawman could see the outlaw sitting on a bench near the center of the musty room. The Indian girl was crouched in the corner beyond.

"Hode—don't move!" Rye shouted as he quickly entered the cabin. "You do and I'll blow your damn head off!"

"You ain't done so good yet," the outlaw yelled back, and surprisingly fast for not only a large man but one who had been wounded, threw himself off the bench and down behind the crude bed nearby.

Rye fired at the outlaw's legs, the only target visible to him. He lunged to one side in the next fragment of time. Wilkinson, seizing his rifle which had been close to the bed, hastily triggered the weapon. The bullet thudded into the wall near the doorway, barely missing Rye and setting up an explosion of dust that merged with the gunsmoke now beginning to fill the cabin.

"On your feet, Hode!" Rye called harshly. "I'm taking you in—alive if possible, dead if you want it that way!"

"Go to hell!" Wilkinson replied. "Ain't no tin star ever took me in and kept me yet!"

"Different this time," the lawman countered, and fired a shot in the direction of the outlaw's voice.

In the murky darkness the lead slug struck the small cook stove standing beyond the bed and sounded a noisy clang. The stovepipe dislodged, fell and sent up a cloud of black soot to further thicken the pall in the room.

Instantly, Rye crouched low, and crossed to the opposite side of the cabin. In the choking mixture of smoke, soot and dust, he dropped down behind a large, dome-lidded trunk—probably once the property of some luckless pilgrim who had run afoul of Wilkinson.

"Warning you again—don't move!" the marshal shouted through the haze.

He could see the outlaw sprawled on the floor by the makeshift bed. Apparently the big mountain man had not seen him cross the room, thanks to the thick gloom. At the sound of the lawman's voice Wilkinson, a blurred, vague shape in the murk near the bed, whipped up his rifle and got to his feet. Rye was reluctant to shoot, and dropped back a step. He came up against the wall as the limping bulk of Hode Wilkinson staggered toward him. His free hand came in contact with the smooth handle of a tool of some kind—an ax. The lawman seized it, brought it up, and with the flat of the blade forward, struck out at the oncoming man.

The blow landed on the side of the outlaw's head with a dull clang. He paused in mid-step, sagged and fell heavily. Rye dropped the ax, rolled the outlaw onto his belly, and drawing the extra pair of chain cuffs he had taken from his saddlebags, linked Wilkinson's thick wrists together. At that moment Rye became aware of a darkening in the doorway. Moving quickly to one side, he leveled his .45 at the cabin's entrance. He swore softly and relaxed. It wasn't the Kiowas, it was Dixie Oliver.

"Damn!" he muttered, and then as she called out anxiously through the obscurity, answered, "I'm all right. Come on in. See what you can do for the girl."

Dixie rested the old double-barreled shotgun she was holding against the wall beside the doorway and entered the cabin. She hesitated uncertainly, repelled by both the fetid odor of the room itself and the dust- and soot-laden cloud of gunsmoke. Glancing about, she located the Indian girl crouched in a back corner, and hurried to her.

The lawman rose and took the arm of the moaning Hode Wilkinson and dragged him to the bed. "Sit down," he ordered. "This time I'm going to tie you so's you won't get away."

Three stained bandages of ragged cloth inexpertly applied indicated the outlaw's previous wounds. One was in the shoulder, another in the fleshy part of his left leg and a third in his right forearm—none of which seemed to have hindered the big man but little.

"I'll be getting away all right," the outlaw muttered slowly, his senses still muddled. "Always have."

"Not this time," Rye countered. Picking up a coil of rope lying on the floor nearby, he fashioned a loop at one end and dropped it about the outlaw's neck, then cut the hemp to proper length and knotted it around one of Wilkinson's ankles. "Try running now and you'll save the territory the cost of hanging you," Rye said as he stepped back.

"It won't hold me," Wilkinson declared stubbornly. "Ain't nothing can hold me."

"Maybe," Rye replied and turned as Dixie came up with the girl.

Dirty, bruised, her dark hair a tangled mass, Morning Sky wore one of Wilkinson's shirts. Her moccasins were in shreds and her feet filthy and covered with sores.

"Just look what he's done to her," Dixie said. "The poor thing, she's sick and starving. He must have treated her like a dog—worse even!"

Rye again drew his knife, and bending down, cut the length of rawhide rope knotted about the Indian girl's ankle. The opposite end, he noted, was nailed to the floor near the fireplace which, judging from the trash and other litter piled in its opening, had not been used in some time.

"And tied up like a dog," he heard Dixie add in a low, angry voice.

Rye looked at the Kiowa girl critically. "She can't do any traveling like she is. Can you fix her up?"

Dixie frowned. "I don't have hardly any clothes with me, but I'll find something. She ought to be washed off."

"That can wait," Rye said. "We need to get away from here fast. Those shots could have been heard by her Indian friends."

Dixie nodded her understanding and turned to the girl. "Come. Clothes—you need something to wear."

Morning Sky appeared to understand, evidently having learned a few words of English, and followed Dixie out into the yard where the mare with the sacks of her possessions was tied.

Rye swung his attention back to the outlaw. "It goes against the grain but I reckon I'll have to fix up that shoulder of yours, too, before you can travel," he said. "As soon not, but they want you alive."

Rye removed the bandage, crusted with dried blood, while Wilkinson cursed steadily. Ignoring the outlaw, the lawman took up a bottle of whiskey that was standing near the head of the bed, removed the cork and poured it liberally over the shoulder wound as well as the two other places where the outlaw had been shot. Wilkinson cursed and squirmed as the alcohol bit into his flesh. Rye ignored it all, and removing his bandanna, snapped it to remove any dust, after which he wound it about the outlaw's shoulder and tied it tight. Wilkinson cursed roundly.

Rye grinned. "You've been doing a good job hurting people for a long time. Maybe you can get a little idea of what it's like," he said, and jerking Wilkinson to his feet, pointed to the door. "Move out."

The outlaw cursed, stumbled forward. "Damn you—I can't walk. That rope—"

"It's staying right where it is," the lawman cut in. "Take short steps, like a hobbled horse. It's not far to that lean-to where you left the white."

Wilkinson cursed again and began to make his way toward the door in short, mincing steps. Several times he almost fell. Rye made no effort to assist the outlaw, but simply watched in stony silence as he waited for the mountain man to regain his balance.

"I'll get loose and I'll kill you for this," Wilkinson grumbled as they moved out into the yard.

"First you'll have to get loose," Rye said dryly. "And I don't aim to let that happen."

They reached the lean-to. Dixie was there with Morning Sky. They had found a little rainwater in a nearby trough and the Indian girl had washed her face and hands, improving her appearance considerably, but fatigue and the harsh treatment by the outlaw were still much in evidence.

The dress Dixie had provided—the only one she had salvaged from the cabin and had intended to wear when she reached a town and went in search of a job—was now on the Indian girl. Several sizes too large, it hung limply from her slight frame but it did cover her nakedness.

"She needs it worse than I do," Dixie said at Rye's show of surprise. "Anyway, I can buy me another one when we get to some town."

"Looks real fetching," the lawman said, loosening the rope connecting Wilkinson's ankles. "Hold that shotgun on my prisoner while I get him into his saddle." Rye paused, glanced about as Dixie hesitated. "We need to move fast," he added impatiently. "Those Kiowas are sure to be around close."

At once Dixie took up the double-barrel and cocking one of the tall, rabbit-ear hammers, leveled it at the outlaw.

"Sure pleasure me some if he'd try to get away," Dixie said. "I owe him plenty for killing Zeb."

Wilkinson turned his head aside and spat. "Go right ahead, girl, and pull the trigger if it'll make you feel better."

"It would, thinking about him and Morning Sky here, and what you've done to her. But I'll wait. I'll get my pleasure from seeing you hanging from the end of a hangman's rope."

When he had gotten Wilkinson's ankles free, Rye assisted the outlaw into the saddle of his horse. Taking the loose end of the rope, he ran it under the white gelding's belly and secured it about the outlaw's opposite ankle.

There was no possibility now that Wilkinson could get off his horse.

"Pick out a mount for the girl," Rye said, starting to remove the grub sacks and the like from Dixie's mare. "We'll use that black for a pack animal. Hurry."

Dixie nodded. Taking the Kiowa girl by the hand, she pointed to the remaining horses and made her understand she was to choose one. Morning Sky immediately crossed to a slim, wiry-looking pinto. Gathering up the dress she was wearing, she expertly swung up onto the pony's back.

By that time Rye had the pack horse ready, and was connecting the animals by a single lead rope. He was working fast. Wolf Killer and the other braves could be somewhere on the far side of the mountain, or they could be among the nearby trees and closing in. There was no way of knowing which. One thing Rye did know for certain was that he did not intend to wait around and find out.

Fourteen

RYE CONSIDERED Hode Wilkinson thoughtfully as the small cavalcade wound its way down the mountain. The big outlaw had been wounded in three places, not counting the blow to the head that had rendered him briefly unconscious. Any one of the injuries would have seriously hampered an ordinary man, perhaps even brought death, but Wilkinson bore them all as if only a minor inconvenience.

Rye had often wondered why some men turned to killing and being an outlaw. There were many reasons, he knew; a man's environment had much to do with it and he suspected such was the reason that had turned Wilkinson from the straight path of abiding the law. Curious, Rye spurred up beside the mountain man, who sat half crouched in his saddle to lessen the pressure of the rope around his neck.

"None of my business," the lawman said, "but I got to thinking you'd make a hell of a good lawman. What made you go the other way?"

Wilkinson turned slowly in his saddle. The bruise on the

side of his head left by the ax was darker, and a bit of
dried blood crusted the corner of his mouth.

"You're damn right—it ain't none of your business,"
the outlaw snapped. "When are you taking this rope off
my neck? It's choking me."

Rye shrugged, glanced around the slopes. So far there
had been no sign of the Kiowas. "Rope comes off when I
see you locked up in a jail."

The lawman looked ahead at the women leading the
party. Dixie was first, followed by Morning Sky. Next in
line was Wilkinson, after whom came Rye, the pack horse
and the trio of extra mounts.

"Why you asking about me?" Wilkinson said after a
time.

"Nothing special. Just came to me that a mighty good
man had gone to waste."

A magpie shot out of the brush on their right, and little
more than knee high above the ground, streaked for a
small meadow farther down the slope.

Wilkinson watched the black and white bird until it had
disappeared, and then turned to Rye. "Hell, Marshal, you
don't know what it's like to be a freak like me—folks
always turning away from you, being a'scared of you just
because you're big. Reckon I might as well be all covered
with poison ivy or something."

There was probably more in the background of Hode
Wilkinson than just size, Rye guessed, but he saw no point
in pursuing it. "There are a lot of big men in this country."

"Yeh? You ever run across one big as me?"

Rye was quiet for a few moments. "No, can't say that I
have."

"I suspect that answers your question," Wilkinson said,
and lapsed into a grim silence.

Rye dropped back into line. He had no particular interest in Hode Wilkinson other than a lawman's curiosity as to what had gone wrong for the man. Something other than his great size had set him on a self-destructive path. He was a cold-blooded killer and a thief, and he and men like him had but one destination in life—a hangman's gallows. Rye had yet to see one who did not deserve it.

They drew near Brimtown well after noon. Dixie swung back to the lawman's side. She looked fresh, and despite the faded, made-over clothing that had once been Zeb Oliver's, she seemed happy and there was a sort of glow about her. This was due, no doubt, to the fact that she was finally getting her wish to leave the lonely life in the mountains that she had come to hate.

"Do I remember you saying you wanted to miss Brimtown?"

Rye nodded. "Could run into trouble there. Too, those Kiowas might be hanging around hoping I'll come by with Wilkinson. Was there that I first came up against them."

"I see. You want to pull up somewhere and eat a bite?"

"Let's go another hour. The Indian girl giving you any trouble?"

"No, she just goes along never making a sound. I guess she'll be glad to get back among her people and the brave she's going to marry."

"Maybe. Some tribes just sort of turn against one of their women who has been used by an outsider."

Dixie straightened up indignantly. "Why? It wasn't her fault! That outlaw caught her, took her by force. It certainly was against her will."

"I know all that but they look at things differently. Now, it could be the Kiowa people aren't like that—but don't bet on it."

"Well, it's sure not fair!" Dixie declared, still in the

throes of indignation. "Do you think those braves are still somewhere close by?"

"I'm sure of it. Best we keep our eyes open. It might be better if you and the girl rode in the back of the line."

"No, I'll stay where I am," Dixie said, and drumming the mare in the ribs with her heels, resumed her place at the head of the string.

Rye would have felt better exchanging places with the young woman, but he supposed, if the Kiowas attacked, one spot would be as good as another. One thing, he had warned her again about the braves; perhaps she would now keep a sharper watch for them.

They rode on steadily, bearing southeast down the slopes of the towering mountain. They halted around midafternoon for a quick lunch of bread, dried meat and water. Coffee was out of the question as smoke might be seen or smelled by the braves if they were in the vicinity. And the lawman had a feeling that they were.

John Rye was not a man to ignore an inner warning. He had kept himself alive through the years by always heeding his intuition, and now with a hated and dangerous outlaw on his hands, not to mention the Kiowa girl the three braves were searching for, he reckoned he had full right to be cautious. Morning Sky, to his way of thinking, didn't really matter. He needed only to see her back to her people.

Hode Wilkinson was something else. Rye, personally, was charged with bringing in the outlaw to face justice, and that came first. He could only hope that the braves would take the girl, should they meet, and let it end there, but Rye knew that was out of the question even as he thought of it. The Kiowas would demand vengeance on Hode Wilkinson whether the girl meant anything to them or not. If he could just be lucky enough to reach Springtown without encountering the braves he could then get Dixie Oliver off his hands and be on his way to Cimarron with his prisoner should he elect to do so.

Near dark and well beyond Brimtown Rye called a halt beside a small stream. There still had been no sign of the Kiowas, and as both women were showing signs of exhaustion, he believed it best to pull up for the night. Also, despite his contempt for the outlaw, he realized the man's wounds should be properly cared for if he were to be alive when they reached their destination, whichever it might be.

Dismounting, he drew Dixie aside. "I don't figure this is very smart but we've got no choice. If you'll get some grub together, I'll look after the horses—and the prisoner."

Dixie nodded wearily. "Is it all right to build a fire?"

"Go ahead," Rye replied as he began to loosen the rope that bound the outlaw to his horse. "We'll be needing hot water to clean up Wilkinson's wounds—and some coffee would sure go good." He hesitated, put his attention on Morning Sky. She was still on her horse. "You been able to talk to her any, make her understand we're taking her back to her people?"

"No. I've tried a couple of times and got nowhere. She doesn't have any use for white folks. I don't think we realize what a bad time she had with him," Dixie added, nodding at Wilkinson.

"Expect it was pretty tough. Maybe she'll get the idea after a couple of days that all whites aren't bad. Think you can get her to help with fixing up some supper?"

"I'd rather take care of it myself," Dixie said, and turned away.

Rye finished releasing Hode Wilkinson from his horse, but left the rope attached to the man's legs along with the loop about his neck, and led the outlaw to a nearby tree.

"Sit down," he ordered, and when Wilkinson complied, tied him securely to the big pine.

"How about my hands?" Wilkinson demanded. "You going to leave them cuffed like they are? Them things are too tight and they hurt—and I sure won't be able to eat."

"Time comes I'll switch them around," the lawman replied.

Wilkinson cursed, "Hell! I've got a right to—"

"Far as I'm concerned you've got no rights at all," Rye cut in. He collected the reins of the horses and led them to a place along the creek below camp where he allowed them to drink. When they had slaked their thirst he took them back to a patch of grass he'd noticed earlier, and securing the animals to a rope strung between two pines, returned to camp.

Dixie had a blackened coffeepot balanced over the flames of a fire and was busy slicing salt pork, potatoes and onions into a frying pan. In a small stew pan some sort of greens were already simmering while on the flat rocks surrounding the fire biscuits were warming.

"Smells mighty good," Rye said, and cast a look at Morning Sky. "Still no help from her?"

"Like I said I don't want any from an Indian. Not sure what she might put in the food." Dixie nodded at Wilkinson. "You might be able to get her to clean him up a bit and doctor his wounds. Knows how—she did fix the ones from the shooting that night in the cabin."

Rye said doubtfully, "Can try. Expect I'll wind up doing it myself. Have we got any kind of disinfectant or salve?"

"In my saddlebags," the young woman replied, and re-

sumed her preparations of the evening meal. "Be some
rags there for bandages, too."

Rye heated a bit of water and crossed to where the
outlaw was seated. Once there he beckoned to Morning
Sky. She gave no indication that she had even seen the
gesture. The lawman shrugged, obtained the medicine and
bandages from Dixie's saddlebags and returned to the outlaw.

"Aim to clean those bullet wounds up a bit," he said,
"and put some medicine on them. Sure don't want them
to get infected."

Wilkinson said nothing, simply continued to stare off
into the darkness. Somewhere close by an owl hooted and
in the creek a fish flapped as it rose to take an insect
floating on the surface. Coyotes were sending their discordant wails higher up on the mountain. The sounds were
all reassuring to the lawman—an indication there was no
one else in the area.

The outlaw made no comment as Rye cleansed the
wounds after removing the bandages. But then he said,
"What're you putting on them bullet holes?"

"Disinfectant first and then some salve."

"I don't want none of that. Tell the Indian to go get
some herb leaves. I don't trust that stuff you've got."

Rye beckoned again to Morning Sky. He pointed to the
outlaw's wounds. "Get some medicine leaves for them."

Morning Sky shook her head.

"He wants your medicine, not mine," Rye continued.

The Indian girl bared her teeth in a mirthless smile.
There was a wild sort of beauty to her. She had pulled her
black hair back over her head. Her dark eyes glittered
angrily while her light brown skin looked golden in the
firelight.

"You go hell," she said, and spat in Wilkinson's be-whiskered face.

The outlaw cursed, lunged at the girl, but the ropes binding him held firm. Lifting his gaze to her, he said something in a terse Indian tongue. Morning Sky laughed jeeringly and moved away.

"Didn't know you spoke the language," Rye said, and went back to dressing the outlaw's wounds.

"There's a hell of a lot you don't know," Wilkinson shot back, squirming a bit as the lawman liberally applied the disinfectant.

"Know I'm going to get you to town for hanging," Rye said dryly. After finishing up the job, he returned Dixie's medicine to her saddlebags and then crossed to the fire. Taking up a cup he poured himself a measure of coffee. The salt pork stew was almost done as were the greens, and their smell filled the small clearing with a pleasant odor.

"Sure makes me realize how hungry I am," he said.

A pleased smile parted Dixie's lips. "Potatoes may be a little hard. Never got a chance to boil them ahead of time." She glanced at Wilkinson. "How's he doing?"

"All right far as I know. Expect a little grub will do him some good."

"Her, too," Dixie said, jerking a thumb at the Kiowa girl sitting sullenly, back to a tree, a few paces away. "You try to be nice to some people and all you get is a cold look."

"I reckon we can't blame her much after what she went through with Wilkinson. She seems to know a little English."

"Maybe so, but we haven't treated her like he did. She's got no reason to hate us. What makes you think she knows some of our language? I tried it on her and got no response, but there were times when I was sure she understood what I was saying to her."

"That's probably all there is to it—she understands a little. And as far as hating us, that's to be expected. Up to now she's probably never been treated decent by any of our kind."

Dixie turned away, began to dish up the food onto the tin plates they had brought along. She was one short since she hadn't anticipated feeding the Kiowa girl, but she improvised by taking her meal directly from the skillet and stew pan.

When the meal was finished Rye spread blankets for the women and himself and tossed one to the outlaw. Wilkinson, his hands in front of his body but still cuffed, caught the woolen cover and wordlessly drew it over himself. The lawman then made a final check of the horses and returned to the camp. The Indian girl was already under the blanket. She looked up at him as he passed, fear and defiance in her eyes as if she were expecting treatment similar to that Wilkinson had accorded her. But the marshal merely glanced at her and made his way on to his own bed.

Rye had not missed the look Morning Sky had given him. He supposed he could not blame her for how she now felt about white men, but he felt he couldn't be saddled with the job of trying to change her attitude. He'd let someone else do that; he had his hands full with Hode Wilkinson and the need to get the outlaw to a secure jail somewhere.

Rye's thoughts came to an abrupt halt. His eyes had caught movement in the brush off to the left of the camp. Possibly it was a deer or some other animal but he couldn't be sure. Twice before that day as they came down the trail he'd had the feeling others were riding along parallel but at a distance from them. He had investigated, found no one. Such had left him unconvinced, however. It had to be the Kiowas waiting for an opportunity to strike.

Gun in hand, the lawman settled down in his blanket. There would be little sleep for him that night, he realized, for if the Kiowas made their move he would need to be ready for them.

Fifteen

"THOSE KIOWA BRAVES are keeping an eye on us," Rye said quietly to Dixie the next morning as they were preparing the early meal. "Spotted somebody in the brush last night. Had to be them."

Dixie paused as she set the coffeepot over the fire. She didn't seem particularly alarmed, probably because of the confidence she had in the lawman. It had been that way with her since that first day she met him.

"You reckon they're planning to attack us?"

Rye tossed another handful of dry wood into the flames as he glanced around. He saw nothing that disturbed him and let his eyes settle on Wilkinson. He was awake. He sat motionless, back to the tree, staring at the marshal with baleful, hate-filled eyes. Morning Sky had also awoken and as Rye shifted his attention to her, she came to a sitting position, threw the blanket aside and began to run fingers through her coal-black hair.

"Hard to figure what Indians will do," Rye said. "My guess is they're just hanging around waiting for us to get closer to their village or camp."

Dixie began to slice salt pork into the spider. "Are we anywhere near that—the village or the camp, I mean?"

Rye shook his head. "Sure don't know the answer to that but my guess is that we're not. We haven't come to the road that turns to Springtown yet and I expect their camp is beyond that."

"Can't we just let her go, let her find her own way back to her people?"

"Been hoping she'd do that, and I've given her plenty of chance, but so far she's stuck with us. Not sure why. Maybe the Indians that've been hanging around aren't Kiowas."

"They are," Hode Wilkinson said, breaking his silence. "They ain't ready to jump you yet, that's all."

The lawman had not been aware that Wilkinson was listening, but he supposed the outlaw hadn't heard anything that he shouldn't have.

"What're they holding back for?"

Wilkinson shrugged his massive shoulders. Rye had left him handcuffed, with a rope about his ankles that was further looped about the mountain man's thick neck and then secured to the tree against which he was sitting. There was little doubt he had spent an uncomfortable night but that meant nothing to Rye.

"Waiting for the rest of the bunch to show up. You'll have more redskins in your hair than a dog's got fleas once they join up."

Rye added more fuel to the low cooking fire. "You're forgetting it's you they're after, not us," he said dryly.

The outlaw laughed. "Hell! Them's Kiowas we're talking about. All whites look alike to them. They hate them all!"

Morning Sky had risen, was now on her feet and rolling her blanket. The dress Dixie had given her no longer had a starched, pressed look but was now wrinkled and soiled, and showed a grease streak where she had wiped her hands while eating. The girl still showed the effects of her time as prisoner with Wilkinson. The bruises on both sides of her face had lightened some but the marks on her neck and arms, and likely the rest of her slender body, were an ugly brown.

Dixie noted her condition and sighed deeply. "Poor thing. She must have had a terrible time . . . And that dress. It was right pretty once."

"Was mighty nice of you to give her that dress," Rye said. "Seemed Hode didn't care whether she had any clothes or not—just let her run around half naked. Expect she had some real cold nights."

"I kept her warm," the outlaw said. "Anyways, there was some buffalo hides laying around the cabin—a couple of wool blankets, too."

"Wasn't wearing anything but one of your old cotton shirts when we first saw her, and it wasn't much more than rags."

"Don't go faulting me for that," Wilkinson protested. "Like I done told you, there was plenty of robes and blankets she could've put on."

Morning Sky had walked off toward the stream. Kneeling beside it, she cupped her hands and bathed her face. After a few minutes she returned to the fire, this time carrying an armload of wood.

Dixie looked up at her in surprise. It was the first time the Kiowa girl had made any effort to help around the camp.

"Obliged to you," she said.

Morning Sky only shrugged and moved over to a fallen tree to sit down. Rye, noting the incident, crossed to where the horses were tethered and gave each a brief going-over. They appeared to be in good condition considering the forage they had been on. When they got to Springtown he'd see that they were all grained. He would also buy a small sack of oats for the continuing journey.

Dixie had a breakfast of corn cakes, fried pork and coffee ready when he returned, and he sat down on the log beside Morning Sky to eat his portion. He was hungry, and for the first time the Kiowa girl ate as if she enjoyed the food. Wilkinson, too, cleaned his plate quickly without his usual grumbling.

"Do you live around here?" Rye asked Morning Sky.

She shook her head, touched her lips with a forefinger to indicate she did not understand. Wilkinson laughed and strained at the bonds that held him prisoner.

"You ain't going to get nothing out of her," he said. "Was you to loosen this here rope, I can maybe find out what you're wanting to know. I talk a little of their lingo."

"Not that important," Rye said, and held out his cup as Dixie approached with the coffeepot.

He glanced at the sky. It was going to be another fine day, warm now that the sun was on its way. Few clouds marred the brilliant blue and only the faintest of breezes stirred through the trees. Small, sparrow-like kinglets were flitting noisily in and out of the brush and a rustling of last winter's dry leaves beneath a nearby clump of mountain ragwort indicated the rooting about of some small animal.

Wilkinson pulled against his bonds. "Just you suit yourself, Mister Lawman. You're a far piece from the Kiowas and damn near as far from any town. You aim to keep me tied up like this till we get there?"

"All the way," Rye said flatly. "You'll be in jail in Springtown before I take off that rope and those cuffs."

A sly look crossed Wilkinson's whiskery face. "That the jail you're putting me in?"

"Maybe. First want to see if it's good enough. If it's not, I'm taking you on to Cimarron. They've got a new jail."

Wilkinson spat and tossed his tin cup toward Dixie, who was standing near the dying fire collecting dishes that were to be cleaned in the stream.

"New or old, it won't hold me," he said.

Rye smiled. "Could be you'll be in for a surprise this time."

Rising, the lawman crossed to Dixie and began to assist her. He felt a hand on his arm. Morning Sky was beside him. She took the pans from him and started toward the creek. Dixie smiled broadly.

"I'll declare, Marshal, but I think she's fallen in love with you!"

"Hardly that," Rye said indifferently. "Expect she's figuring that helping a bit will get her home a little sooner."

"She won't ever get home," Wilkinson said, "and we ain't never going to reach Springtown neither. Them savages are just honing to take our hair."

Dixie shuddered. Rye, staring off into the brush where he thought he had seen movement, shrugged. "Long as we've got Morning Sky we've got something to bargain with."

"Only you ain't got her no more," the outlaw said with a smirk. "She's gone."

Rye wheeled, glanced hurriedly about. Morning Sky was nowhere to be seen. Dixie uttered a low cry.

"When—how—"

"When you was jabbering busy-like," Wilkinson said. "Took the horse she was riding, too."

Rye's anger mounted. "If you saw her leave why the hell didn't you sing out?"

Wilkinson shrugged. "Weren't no skin off my backside."

"Wrong there," the lawman stated. "We had something to make a deal with. Now we've got nothing except you—and it's you they want."

"You're forgetting your woman there. Them braves will take a big fancy to her."

Rye made no reply but moved quickly to Dixie. "We best get out of here fast. Morning Sky's leaving means the rest of the Kiowas are around close," he said tersely. "Forget what you're doing, get set to pull out. I'll bring up the—"

Rye's words broke off. He felt his nerves tighten as a sudden sense of immediate danger swept through him. He saw Dixie Oliver's expression change, saw her eyes widen and her mouth become a taut line. His hand dropped to the gun on his hip as he spun—and slowly fell away.

Standing at the edge of the clearing were a half-dozen painted braves. Among them were Wolf Killer and Little Horse. More Kiowas had encircled the camp.

Sixteen

ONE OF THE KIOWAS, clad in white cotton pants, no shirt and wearing a feathered headdress, said something in a loud voice and pointed at Wilkinson. Two of the braves broke from the group and crossed quickly on moccasined feet to where the outlaw sat tied to the tree. One drew a knife from his belt and hunched before him.

"No!" Rye called out sharply. "That man is a prisoner of the United States Government. Don't take him or you will become outlaws, too."

The brave with the knife paused. He turned to the one with the headdress, shrugged and then proceeded to cut the rope that held Wilkinson to the tree as well as the end binding his ankles. Taking the outlaw's hands, he held them aloft to show the manacles. At that point Wolf Killer stepped forward.

"Give him the key to unlock the iron cuffs."

Rye did not move. Anger was coursing through him, stiffening his big frame and tugging at the muscles of his hard-set face. Wolf Killer had changed. What small reasonableness the lawman had thought he detected at their first meeting was no longer evident. Wolf Killer turned to the feathered brave and spoke rapidly in his guttural language. At the response he received, he turned to the marshal.

"Running Dog says you are to give Gray Deer the key. If you do not One Ear will die here. Also you and your woman will die. Those are the words of Running Dog, a chief."

Rye realized that against such odds he could not possibly win, but stubbornness and his sense of duty would not permit him to give in.

"Who is this Chief Running Dog? I have heard of Big Tree and White Bear, the one we call Satanta, but Running Dog is not known to me—and I know many chiefs. Is he just a subchief?"

"It does not matter," Wolf Killer replied. "He is a warrior chief of the Kiowas. One Ear is our prisoner as are you and your woman. In Kiowa country our law is first."

Rye glanced at Dixie. Arms folded across her breasts, she appeared to be unafraid, a pretense of support for him, he knew. He smiled, hoping to reassure her.

"This is not Kiowa land. Kiowa land is farther east."

"You do not speak true!" Little Horse shouted, coming into the conversation. A bit of cloth was wrapped loosely about his shoulder. The bullet he had fired hastily had inflicted but minor damage, Rye thought. "The Kiowas ride far. They have much land."

"It is you who does not speak true words," the lawman said calmly. "You were given a reservation to the east by my chiefs where you could live in peace with other tribes and the soldiers."

"What they did is of no importance. The Kiowas choose their own trails and their own way of life. At Adobe Walls we showed we have no fear. At other places, too. We are not afraid of the whites and your soldiers."

"Adobe Walls was a long time ago. Much has happened since then. Many of your chiefs are dead and some are yet in the white man's jails. It is foolish for you to bring trouble upon your people by defying my government and taking my prisoner from me. Tell Running Dog that, and if you—"

Rye hesitated. One of the warriors, a strapping young buck wearing only a breechcloth, had moved over to Dixie and was looking her over with obvious admiration. The sun was well up by then and the Kiowa's lithe body shone bright copper in the strong light. He said something to the other braves, and laughing, reached out and laid a hand on the young woman's arm. Dixie recoiled. The lawman reacted immediately.

"Tell that brave," he said to Wolf Killer, "that if he touches my woman again I will kill him."

Wolf Killer was silent for several moments and then repeated the warning to the Kiowa. The brave drew back, glaring at Rye while he gestured threateningly with the rifle he held. Running Dog spoke sharply. The young Kiowa turned sullenly and rejoined the group with the chief.

"Have a care!" Little Horse shouted. "It is you who will be killed! You are—"

Running Dog spoke. At that Little Horse fell silent. The war chief gestured at Wolf Killer and barked an order. The brave nodded and crossing to the lawman, searched his vest for the key to Wilkinson's cuffs. After holding it aloft for all to see, he tossed it to Gray Deer.

Again Running Dog spoke in his sharp way. Wolf Killer turned back to Rye and jerked the lawman's pistol from its holster. Anger flared through Rye. He lunged at the Kiowa in an effort to reclaim the weapon. The clicking of several rifles being cocked brought him up short. Dixie hurried to his side.

"No!" she said anxiously.

Rye shrugged. It was a foolish move on his part, he told himself. Best wait for an opportunity to recover his weapon and escape when the odds weren't so long. He nodded to Wolf Killer.

"Tell Running Dog this will bring him big trouble. I am a lawman, a United States Marshal. When I report this to my chief in Washington he will send the soldiers back. There will be much killing."

"Faw!" Little Horse spat. "Killing does not matter! We are Kiowas. Much land was taken from us by your General Sheridan many years ago. All that is as water down a river. Today it is different. The Kiowas are strong."

Rye shook his head. "Your talk is of no worth. It is Running Dog who must decide. He is chief."

Little Horse stood motionless while the remaining braves stirred restlessly. The lawman shifted his attention to Wolf Killer.

"Your brother has angry blood. You tell Running Dog what I have said."

The brave nodded as the tense silence held. Finally he turned to Running Dog and in short, jerky spurts, translated what the lawman had said. When he had finished, the chief shrugged and made a brief reply. Wolf Killer swung his attention back to Rye.

"Running Dog says this will be decided tomorrow. We return to our camp now." Glancing about, he spoke to the braves near him, and they in turn faded into the brush where their horses were picketed. Shortly a Kiowa appeared leading the horses Rye, Dixie and Wilkinson were riding, and motioned for them to mount.

"Stick close to me," the lawman said to Dixie. "We've got no choice except to go along with them now and hope something turns up later."

Hode Wilkinson, roped to the saddle of his white horse, swore. "Ain't nothing good going to turn up, you can bet your last copper on that."

Rye's shoulders twitched. "Maybe. But best you wait and see. I still aim to get you to Cimarron or maybe Santa Fe for hanging. Fact is, Springtown will do if you give me any trouble."

The braves had all crawled up onto their ponies. Running Dog motioned for all to move out, indicating by grunts and gestures that they were to follow Wolf Killer and Little Horse.

The lawman, with Dixie close by, swung into the line of half-naked riders. There was little else they could do at the moment. Once they reached the Kiowa camp there was a chance he could convince Running Dog and any other chiefs who might be present, through Wolf Killer, that they were making a serious mistake. The white man's government had first claim on Hode Wilkinson, he would tell them, and it was best they stay out of it. Just how successful he would be was a matter of conjecture, but there would be nothing lost in trying.

Failing to convince the Kiowas that Wilkinson would be punished for his crimes against both whites and Indians no doubt would be difficult, that was easy to see.

They rode on through the day in a double line at times, in single file at others, always with Rye, the young woman and Hode Wilkinson well guarded. Twice the young brave who had taken a fancy to Dixie dropped back and rode beside her. He made no attempt to touch her, however, but that was of little comfort to the girl. Night lay ahead and she felt she could expect the worst from the Kiowa then.

They halted at a small stream at the edge of a broad

plain that extended indefinitely to the south. Before they could dismount, Wolf Killer came to them.

"You will not dismount. We go on soon."

Several braves took charge of Wilkinson at that point, tightening the rope they had put around him, poking and prodding him with their rifles to force the huge mountain man to do their bidding.

"What are we supposed to do?" Dixie wondered as she crowded the mare up close to Rye's buckskin.

"We wait," the lawman said flatly, watching the braves hustle Wilkinson off to one side. "Probably aim to rest a spell, then go on and make night camp."

Rye felt her fingers press into his forearm. "I—I want to thank you for saying what you did when that Indian put his hand on me. What did he mean by it?"

"He was telling the other braves that you are his captive —his slave—so they wouldn't try to claim you."

Dixie shuddered. "I'll kill myself before I let him or any of the others take me—and if I'm where I can't, I want your promise to shoot me."

"It won't come down to that," the lawman said. "I'll see to it."

Over to the right where the braves had taken the outlaw a yell of pain went up. Rye shook his head.

"They've already started working on him. For what he did to them, I reckon he's got it coming."

"Will they kill him?"

"Doubt it, leastwise not here. They'll take him to their camp or village." Rye paused, rubbed at the stubble on his jaw. "I've got to somehow get him away from them."

"What's the difference in them punishing him and the law doing it? He'll pay with his life either way."

"The law is the law of the land. If we don't see that it comes first and is obeyed and respected by everybody, we might as well quit because the outlaws will take over and it'll be men like Hode Wilkinson running everything."

Dixie's shoulders stirred in a helpless gesture. "I don't see how you can do anything. I'm wondering if either one of us will get out of it alive."

Rye smiled grimly. "Don't give up. There's a chance we'll make it to green grass yet."

Seventeen

THEY RODE OUT a half hour later bearing steadily northeast. There seemed to be no great hurry and they traveled leisurely across the flats and later, the diminishing hills. Rye had hoped without much enthusiasm that they would encounter a party of prospectors or hunters, or even cowhands, that he could somehow enlist in his need to recover Wilkinson, but they saw no one or no thing other than a high-flying eagle soaring lazily in the blue sky, totally disinterested in the humans crawling across the land below it.

"They didn't do much to Wilkinson," Rye said shortly after they got under way. "Means they're saving him for big doings later—probably tonight if we reach camp by then."

Dixie brushed at the moisture on her forehead. She was bearing up well under the ordeal. "Whatever they do I don't want to see it."

"We probably won't. Like as not we'll be treated as prisoners, and when they're finished with Wilkinson, turned loose."

"Do you really think so?"

The lawman nodded. "The Indian tribes are all pretty well civilized and at peace nowadays. They don't put on the war paint unless somebody's wronged them—and Wilkinson sure did that."

Taking Wilkinson from the Kiowas later—if he got the chance—would not be easy, Rye knew, despite his confident words to the young woman. The outlaw would be under guard every moment once they reached the Indian camp, just as he was now with a quartet of braves riding tight around the outlaw's big white horse.

They continued on through the night until near dawn when they broke out of a scatter of brushy hills into a fairly large valley through which a sparkling stream could be seen flowing.

"Not a regular camp," Rye said. "Must have been set up as a sort of base while they hunted for Wilkinson."

There were no more than a half-dozen tipis. No women or dogs were to be seen as they rode toward the cluster of canvas and hide tents. Only two showed smoke issuing from the openings in their tops. There was little brush and only a few trees about the camp.

"Does that mean we'll keep on moving?" Dixie asked wearily. The lawman could see she was near exhaustion.

He shook his head. "Hard to say what they'll do. Could be they'll want to take Wilkinson back to their main village."

"Where would that be?"

"On east, in Kansas probably. But they just might do their punishing right here. We won't know until the time comes."

They reached the edge of the camp and started toward one of the larger tipis standing slightly apart from the others. As they drew near several Kiowa braves came from their shelters to meet them. Some wore paint, all were talking excitedly and pointing at Wilkinson. A few eyed Rye and Dixie Oliver suspiciously.

When they halted before what was apparently the chief's tipi Wolf Killer rode up immediately. He sat quietly on his pony while Running Dog and Little Horse dismounted and entered the shelter. Moments later they reappeared accompanied by a tall, impressive-looking Kiowa man with thick, black shoulder-length hair, small, narrowed eyes and a down-curving mouth.

"I guess he's the big chief," Rye murmured. "Got to try and talk to him." He turned to Wolf Killer. "Who is this Kiowa chief? Can he speak my tongue?"

Wolf Killer shrugged his muscular shoulders. "You will listen well to him. He is the mighty chief Talking Bird. His words are the law of the Kiowa people."

"Does he speak my tongue?" Rye repeated.

Three more braves rode into the camp at full speed and came to a dramatic halt near the chief in a swirl of dust.

"He did not learn the white man's tongue," Wolf Killer said.

Rye swore softly. Attempting to get something done through an interpreter always made things doubly difficult.

"Will you talk for me?" Rye asked, attention still on the old chief standing ramrod straight in the bright sunlight, dark-seamed features impassive.

Talking Bird was wearing a gray and red striped jacket over a faded red shirt. Twin rows of porcupine quills ran down the front of the outer garment, and an old cavalry neckerchief hung loosely about his neck. His pants were old army castoffs as were the knee-high boots gathered in wrinkles about his legs. Many eagle feathers had gone into the making of his headdress, which trailed down well below his middle.

"It will be as Talking Bird wishes," Wolf Killer said.

Rye glanced about at the braves gathered nearby. "Where is Brown Bear? I do not see him."

"That I do not know. Perhaps he has gone back to our village on the Washita."

"Did he take Morning Sky with him?"

"There is no longer to be a marriage between them. Will you speak your words to Talking Bird now or later when the council fires are built?"

"Now."

Wolf Killer rode forward slightly. Most of the party had dismounted and drifted off, leaving only a half-dozen rifle-bearing braves present to take charge of the prisoners. At Wolf Killer's words the chief fixed his stare on Rye. In the morning light his small black eyes were like bits of obsidian. His voice was sharp as he spoke to Wolf Killer.

At that the brave nodded to Rye. "Speak what is in your mind to say. I will translate it to Talking Bird."

The lawman wasted no time but immediately stated what he had said previously—that the Kiowas had no right to take Hode Wilkinson from him, that he was a prisoner of the law and must be surrendered to him, a representative of the government.

Before he had finished his demands Talking Bird was shaking his head and speaking. Wolf Killer listened intently. He was now dressed more like the other braves, in cotton pants, with belt and knife, moccasins, and a strip of cloth about his head. He carried his rifle, a late model lever action, Rye noted, across his legs. When the chief had finished he faced Rye.

"Talking Bird says you have no power on Kiowa land. He will not give One Ear to you. It is the Kiowas' right to punish him for his evil doings."

"Better explain to him that all the land under the sky is

controlled by my chiefs in Washington. He should know that by now. He can't—"

"Talking Bird will not listen," Wolf Killer broke in. "He says to tell you One Ear has done terrible things to our women, to our people, and it is our right to punish him."

"I agree he has done many wrong things to the Kiowas, but it is my government who must punish him."

Wolf Killer conversed with his chief for several moments, emphasizing or explaining some points with gestures. When he had finished he listened to the chief's reply and then translated it to the marshal.

"He says that cannot be, that it was the Kiowas who were wronged, that it was on Kiowa land that it took place, therefore it is the Kiowas that have the right to punish or perhaps kill One Ear."

As the brave spoke, the old chief stood silent, and then, when Wolf Killer had finished, he slapped both hands together in a sliding motion, wheeled and reentered his tipi.

"He will talk no more," Wolf Killer said. "Come. I will take you to the tipi where you are to wait."

The brave turned his pony about and started back across the clearing that lay in the center of the shelters. Only a few braves were to be seen, and Hode Wilkinson was no longer in evidence, having been led off on his white horse several minutes earlier. Rye wondered if the outlaw's punishment had already started or if he had just been taken to one of the tipis where, bound and possibly gagged, he would await the Kiowas' pleasure.

"You will stay here," Wolf Killer said a short time later as they drew up before one of the shelters. "Do not come outside once you have entered. It will not be safe."

"Where have they taken my prisoner?" Rye asked as he and Dixie dismounted. "And where is our pack horse? There are things that will be needed."

"It is no concern of yours where they have taken One Ear. And I do not know what has become of the animal you speak of."

"It is the one that carries our blankets and other things of importance to us."

Wolf Killer shook his head. "I cannot answer for I do not know. Take heed. You will stay inside the tipi. To come out will be of great danger to you," he said, and taking up the reins of the buckskin and Dixie's mare, wheeled and rode toward the far side of the camp.

Rye watched the brave for a few moments, and then pulled back the flap of the tipi. Holding it open, he nodded to the young woman.

"Best we get inside. Only thing we can do for the moment is keep out of sight."

Dixie moved past him into the canvas cone. It was empty except for a pile of hides lying against the opposite wall, and the ashes of a previous fire. Heat was already building inside the shelter as the sun climbed higher, and by noon, Rye reckoned, despite the opening in the top for the poles, it would be nearly unbearable to remain inside.

"Will they bring us something to eat?" Dixie wondered as she sat down on the pile of hides.

"Expect so," Rye answered. He moved back to the flap and drew it carefully aside. "I'd sure like to know where they've taken our horses."

The center of the camp, ringed by most of the tipis, was deserted. It was evident the Kiowas were holding a meeting somewhere, possibly to discuss the fate of Wilkinson, or perhaps they were waiting for more of the tribe to come in. Whatever, the odds that he would be able to get his hands and rope on the outlaw again were long—and growing longer. But John Rye knew he had to try.

Eighteen

THE MORNING WORE ON with the heat inside the tipi rising steadily. No food was brought and twice, when Rye pulled open the flap to call for Wolf Killer and protest the treatment they were being accorded, he was shouted back with threatening gestures accompanied by several rocks that struck the tipi. After the second try he gave it up and sat down on the pile of crackling, dry hides next to Dixie.

"I expect we'll get a bite of grub when they get around to it," he said.

Dixie stirred, made a hopeless motion with her hands. "Everything is for nothing," she murmured. "We're helpless. We have no weapons and there's nobody—like the army—around to help."

Rye thrust a hand into his left boot, drew forth the hunting knife he habitually carried as a reserve weapon.

"Got this," he said.

The young woman's eyes brightened for a moment, and then she shrugged. "What good's a knife? You'll never get close enough to one of those Indians to use it. They're careful," she said despondently.

Rye was surprised. For a woman who had grown up in

the mountains where self-reliance was second nature, she gave up much too easily. Perhaps it was to be expected. She was very tired.

"Never know for sure," the lawman said with a smile. "Just might get a chance."

"I hope so. What are they doing out there?"

"Couldn't tell much about it. Looked like the whole bunch had gathered in front of the chief's tipi."

"Some kind of a meeting I guess," she said tonelessly.

"Probably. Expect it's about Hode."

"Did you see him?"

"Yeh. They've got him tied to a tree close to where the meeting's going on. Looks like they held off working him over. Appears to be in about the same shape as he was when we last saw him. He's a strong man. He can take a lot of punishment."

Dixie shivered. "Looking at him always gives me the creeps." She paused. "It's not very Christian, and Zeb always said I should try to be a good one, but I don't care what they do to him. He killed Zeb, just shot him down without giving him a chance. He deserves whatever the Indians do to him."

"I reckon that will be a'plenty," Rye said, and dug into his inside pocket for one of the black stogies he carried.

It was the last one, but he felt the need for a smoke to clear his head and accelerate the thought process. Somehow he had to escape the vigilant eyes of the Kiowas, free Hode Wilkinson, and with Dixie and the outlaw, make a run for the nearest town, either Cimarron or Springtown, he didn't care which.

He glanced to the rear of the canvas tipi. He could cut a slit in the fabric with this knife large enough to crawl through. After that he and Dixie could make a dash for the nearest brush. That was a hundred yards or so distant, as near as he could recall. With the tipi between them and the gathering of Kiowas in the center of the clearing, they just might make it to a hiding place without being seen. But after that what—

"Marshal . . . John . . ."

He turned to the woman. It was the first time she had called him by his given name. "Yes?"

"I want to tell you . . . thank you . . . for letting them think I'm your woman . . . your wife. I know that's had a lot to do with them leaving me alone."

"Like to think it'll stay that way." He paused as the sound of horses rushing into the camp beat a tattoo on the hard, grassy ground. It could only mean more Kiowas were coming in. "I figured you wouldn't mind me saying it long as it was for a good purpose."

"Mind? No, not at all! It actually sort of made me feel good—being your woman. Fact is, I wouldn't mind at all if it was true."

Rye did not look at the young woman. He'd been through the same problem a few times before when by chance or forced choice he'd found himself with a desirable woman on his hands to look out for.

"Would it be so bad for you—for us—if we—"

"A wife's out of the question for me," the marshal said, trying to bring the discussion to an end before it could go further.

"Why do you say that?"

Rye scrubbed at his jaw. "Well, for one thing, I'd never put a woman through the kind of life I have to lead."

"You mean your being a lawman and on the move all the time. If I could go with you I'd find it exciting."

"But you couldn't, at least not often. And when I was away you'd know nothing but worry—you'd always be expecting something to happen—bad news."

"Other lawmen get married, have a wife—"

"Lawmen of a different kind. They're men who can have a home and seldom need to leave town, like a sheriff or a deputy. My job's different. The closest thing to a home I can claim is a hotel room in Wichita and I don't get a chance to use it more than a half-dozen times a year. When I think about it I reckon my real home is my saddle."

Dixie remained silent. Outside something was happening. Yells were going up and there were sounds of digging mixing with the smell of wood smoke.

One thing was certain in John Rye's mind; he couldn't try to escape without Dixie even though having her along would make the effort doubly difficult. But that was a chance he'd have to take. He'd not leave her behind. If things looked right, he'd wait for dark and then make a break for the brush. Once they reached there he would hide the girl while he somehow managed to get their horses—and Hode Wilkinson.

Free Wilkinson—One Ear—the man the Kiowas hated most of all. That would be the most difficult thing he'd face. He could be sure the Indians, even with the outlaw tied to the tree, would post guards around him. Getting by them would be hard to do—but that was where his knife would come in handy. One thing in his favor, the moon was in its last quarter and he could expect to move about without drawing any attention, assuming he was careful.

The yelling increased. Rye arose and crossed to the tipi's entrance. Carefully drawing back the flap, he looked out. The number of Kiowas seemed to have grown or perhaps other tribes had joined in to punish their common enemy. Hode Wilkinson was no longer tied to a tree at the edge of the camp but was now bound to a pole that had been erected in the center of the clearing. Arms pulled behind him, legs securely trussed, he stood rigidly against the pole like some huge beast from another world—strong, defiant, fearless but a helpless captive nevertheless.

A half-dozen braves, talking among themselves, faced him. One paused, bent down, picked up a fist-sized rock and threw it at the outlaw, striking him in the chest. If Wilkinson felt it he gave no sign.

Rye wondered about the man's wounds, if they were becoming infected due to lack of attention. From that distance he could, of course, tell little about it. The cloth on Wilkinson's shoulder was darkly stained, as was the one on his forearm, but the bandage about his thigh looked different. Rye shook his head; such things mattered little to him. Wilkinson earned what he had sustained. Anyway, he need have no fear for the outlaw's well-being where his wounds were concerned. The Kiowas would use their primitive but effective medical skills to keep the man alive.

"What are they doing?" Dixie had risen and was now standing at his shoulder. "They've moved him—tied him to a pole!"

"Looks like he's going to be the center of attention," the lawman said dryly.

"All that brush piled near him, does that mean they're going to burn him, like they used to do witches?"

"Looks that way . . . Can you spot our horses? I think I can see Wilkinson's white horse over there beyond the chief's tipi."

Dixie studied the area for several moments. She nodded. "Yes, I can see it."

"Not sure it was the horse or something white. I don't see the others, your mare and my buckskin. Can you?"

The young woman, weariness deepening the lines of her face, was silent as she concentrated on the partly visible area beyond Talking Bird's shelter. Finally she shook her head.

"I don't see them either. What do you—"

"My guess is they're with the white along with the pack horse and the others we had. We'll have to take a chance on it, anyway."

Dixie turned her face up to him. "Do you mean we're going to try and escape?"

He nodded. "Just as soon as it's dark." Turning to the pile of hides, he rustled about in them until he found a couple large enough to lie on. "Want you to stretch out and rest. Get some sleep if you can. It won't be the best bed you've ever been on, but it'll beat the hard ground."

Dixie smiled wanly and moved the pallet of horse hides. Dropping upon them, she stretched out, sighing as she ignored the crackling sound. She looked up at the lawman.

"Why don't you lie down beside me? You can use a rest, too."

Rye needed no second invitation, and there was no point in keeping an eye on the Kiowas for the time being.

"Believe I will," he said, and stretched out beside her.

John Rye did not sleep well, but merely dozed. Around mid-afternoon, fully rested and awake, and taking care not to arouse the young woman, he moved carefully off the hides and got to his feet. At once he crossed to the tipi's flap and glanced out.

More Indians were now to be seen, most of whom were squatting on their haunches near the chief's tipi, smoking and talking. Hode Wilkinson was still tied to the pole but he was no longer upright. Now he sagged against the bonds that held him to the stripped tree. He was still alive, and that was what mattered to Rye. As long as the Kiowas and their friends did not kill him, he had a chance to free the outlaw and get him to one of the settlements.

Hunger and thirst were gnawing at him. The hot interior of the tipi with its opening flap closed was almost unbearable and reminded him of the time he'd found himself stranded alone and on foot in the Arizona desert with no food or water, miles from any habitation. He had managed to survive that just as he was determined to live through this and eventually deliver his prisoner as ordered.

Dixie would be suffering, too, he thought as he looked down on her. It had been an ordeal for her from the moment they had been captured by the Kiowas, but she had complained little if at all. Dixie Oliver was one hell of a woman and any man would be proud to ride the river with her.

Rye sat down again, this time on the barren ground after opening the tipi's flap as much as he dared. It not only allowed a bit more air to enter but aided the air trapped inside to more readily escape through the opening for the poles at the top.

Near dark, activity in the camp picked up. Several large fires were built, some for cooking, others to provide light. The Kiowas had killed two deer, quartered them and had the meat roasting over open flames. The odor drifting to Rye was tantalizing and whetted his hunger to the extreme, but there was nothing he could do about it.

Dixie awoke, aroused by the smell of the cooking venison. She smiled ruefully. "To think I got so tired of deer meat that I could hardly stomach it!"

Rye nodded. "Right now I could eat a buck hoof, horns, hide and all! If I—"

There was a faint scratching sound at the rear of the tipi. Shortly a knife blade began to swiftly cut its way through the fabric. Rye came to his feet, and with his own knife drawn, looked hurriedly around. There was nothing else he could use as a weapon, no stick of wood, no rock. He would have to make the best of what he had if the intruder, probably the young buck who had taken a fancy to Dixie, attempted to claim the young woman.

Abruptly the blade disappeared, leaving only a slit in the canvas. A bundle was thrust through it.

"My dress!" Dixie cried as the lawman bent down to take the wadded-up garment. "It must be Morning Sky. She's trying to help us."

The bundle was far heavier than one containing only a woman's dress. Rye unwound it quickly. Several strips of jerky—pemmican he recalled it was often called—dropped to the ground. He continued to unfold the bit of clothing. A quick feeling of hope and thankfulness ran through him. The heavy object was a pistol.

"We've got a weapon now!" Dixie said in a breathless sort of voice. "Now we can—" She broke off. A frown pulled at her features as she stared at Rye. "It's a pistol, isn't it?"

"It's a pistol all right, but a useless one," the marshal replied heavily. "It's an old cap and ball piece that probably hasn't been fired in years. Besides that, there's no ammunition."

Dixie settled back on the hides. "I guess Morning Sky didn't know any better. She was trying to help us, though."

Rye was examining the old weapon thoughtfully. "Maybe she's helped more than you think. We don't have any ammunition but most likely we're the only ones who know that. The gun will probably—"

A rattle of gunshots sounded in the late day. Yells mixed with the pound of running horses and the crackle of rifle fire echoed across the clearing. Rye rushed to the tipi's opening and jerked it back.

Two dozen or so braves were invading the camp. Several of the Kiowas, caught off guard, were down. The rest were scurrying for their shelters, where they had evidently left their weapons. Rye spun, grasped Dixie by the hand and pulled her to her feet.

"Come on! The camp's being raided," he said in a taut voice. "This is our chance to get out of here."

Nineteen

BENT LOW, with the old Colt pistol in his left hand and Dixie Oliver at his heels, Rye hurried through the opening of the tipi into the dust and smoke that were beginning to hang over the clearing.

Riders were swerving back and forth across the open ground lying between the shelters. Several braves lay motionless on the hard ground. A riderless horse galloped by.

"Who are they?" Dixie asked in a strained voice as they hesitated in the shadow of a tipi for breath.

"Could be Arapahos," Rye said, eyes on Hode Wilkinson, who was barely visible through the haze. The outlaw appeared to be all right and was struggling to break the ropes that held him to the pole. "I think we're on their hunting grounds, and they're here to drive the Kiowas out. Or it could be a bunch of renegades after horses and women."

"Women?" Dixie echoed. "There aren't any women here except Morning Sky . . . and me."

"Whoever they are they probably don't know that. Chance, too, they could be Comancheros. I've heard of them coming this far north."

"Comancheros?"

The crackling of rifles and the yelling had increased. Smoke and dust had also thickened. There would come no better time to make a move.

"They're a wild outlaw bunch, mostly Mexican bandidos but you'll find Americans and renegade Indians running with them, too."

Two riders, hunched low over their ponies, rushed by. Each clutched a lever-action repeating rifle in one hand and his pony's mane in the other. They wore only breechcloths, headbands and some kind of knee-high leggings. Wild sounds were coming from their flared mouths, and they seemed bent on a solitary purpose not discernible to Rye.

"Were those Comancheros?" Dixie asked.

"Could have been," the lawman replied. "Stay close to me. I've got to get to Wilkinson."

Moving from shelter to shelter, they came to a point where they were directly opposite the outlaw. The fighting had grown more intense, and the number of shadowy riders and horses had grown. Evidently many of the Kiowas had been able to reach their ponies and were now carrying on the battle on equal footing.

"John—"

At the young woman's word, the lawman looked around. She was pointing at the body of an Indian a few steps away.

"Isn't that—"

"Wolf Killer," Rye answered before she could finish.

The lawman's jaw tightened. He had liked the young brave. Wolf Killer had been one he could talk to and reason with. Unlike Little Horse he was not dead set against all whites because of the murderous actions of a few, but realized there could be outlaws on both sides.

They pressed on, hunched low, taking benefit from the shadows and the smoke and dust. A rider galloped by little more than a wagon's length away. Wearing a battered old narrow-brimmed hat and what looked to have been a blue serge suit now faded to dull gray, he was undoubtedly an American.

"Comancheros for sure," the lawman muttered as he edged forward for a better look at the clearing.

The fighting had not slowed. There was still the steady firing of rifles. The yelling had not slacked off, and the fires continued to blaze brightly. He could see several more bodies on the ground and more riderless horses wandering aimlessly about.

"I aim to make a run for Wilkinson," Rye said. "I'll cut the ropes, then head for the horses over back of the chief's tipi." *If they're still there,* he added to himself. "You can wait here."

Dixie's reply was firm. "No, I'll go with you."

Rye gathered his legs under him and moved out into the clearing. He stopped abruptly, his arm going out to check the young woman's steps. A brave was moving directly toward them from the right. The marshal turned, glanced hurriedly about. The Kiowa could not fail to see them if they remained where they were.

Rye grasped the girl's hand, and again keeping low, headed for the tipi immediately to their left. It would be empty, he realized, as the braves occupying it would all be engaged in the fight with the Comancheros.

Reaching the opening, he moved quickly inside and drew Dixie in behind him. He allowed the flap to fall into place and stepped to one side. He'd give the brave time to pass, then try again to cross to Wilkinson. His one chance to rescue the outlaw would be while the fighting was at its height. If—

Suddenly the tipi's entrance flap was brushed aside. The half-crouched figure of the brave filled the opening. The Kiowa drew up sharply in surprise at the vague sight of the lawman and the young woman. Rye swore and lunged at the man. His luck was anything but good. He had picked the wrong tipi for a hiding place. The brave had come there apparently for something he needed.

A yell broke from the brave's flared mouth as Rye's solid weight crashed into him. The rifle he was holding dropped from his hand as he went down. The lawman's arm swung quickly. The old pistol he held thudded against the brave's head. The Kiowa went limp.

Rye drew back instantly. Thrusting the Colt cap and ball under his belt, he snatched up the rifle the Indian had dropped, and stepped to the tipi's entrance. Pulling aside the flap, he looked carefully around. The sounds of gunfire and the yelling had slackened off but the thick, floating clouds of dust and smoke still hung over the clearing. He reached back and touched the young woman's arm.

"Fighting's about over. We've got to make a run for it. Think you can do it?"

In the flickering, unstable light coming from the fires, the young woman's features looked pale and drawn. She nodded. "I'm ready."

At once Rye, motioning for Dixie to remain low and assuming a like stance himself, moved out into the confused night. Three braves, prostrate shapes sprawled facedown in the clearing just ahead, further attested to the fierceness of the battle, whatever its reason. Whether the Kiowas or the Comancheros were winning Rye had no way of knowing.

Taking a deep breath, and with the comforting weight of the rifle in his hand, Rye ran hard for the pole to which his prisoner was tied, looming up vaguely in the pall.

When he had reached it he dropped to the ground. As Dixie followed his example he looked up at the outlaw.

"Hode, it's Rye."

Wilkinson's head, sunk into his massive chest, roused. "Rye—the marshal?"

"Right. I'm going to cut you loose, then try to get to the horses."

The outlaw had been tied to the pole the full day. His legs would be numb and strength likely gone from them.

"Can you run?"

"Ain't for sure. Don't feel like I've got any legs. That damn rawhide rope—"

Rye had not waited for the outlaw to reply. He had drawn his knife and was slicing through the cords that pinned the man to the pole. Two riders thundered by. They did not slow, evidently not noticing the lawman and the young woman who, at that moment, had stretched out close to the ground.

Wilkinson sagged forward as the last rope was cut. He went to his knees with a curse, and then twisted about to face Rye.

"What're we doing now?" he asked.

Rye pointed to the area behind the chief's tipi. It was partially hidden by another shelter as well as the deep gloom. Cocking the rifle he held, he leveled it at the outlaw.

"Over there. Try to get away from me and I'll kill you."

Wilkinson made no answer but started at a shambling, unsteady run for the area the lawman had indicated. They gained the first tipi and rounded it. A tight grin pulled at Rye's dry lips. The horses, all of them, were still there.

"You get your mare," Rye said to Dixie. "I'll have to look after Wilkinson till we get clear and I can put a rope back on him."

"Are we taking the pack horse?" the young woman asked as she hurried to her horse.

"No, he'd hold us back," he replied, prodding Wilkinson with the end of the rifle barrel.

The outlaw swung stiffly up into the saddle of the white. Rye, collecting the lengths of rawhide rope and cord that had been used on the outlaw, gestured with the rifle.

"Don't forget what I told you about making a wrong move," he warned as he mounted.

Wilkinson only shrugged. "We ain't going to get far," he said. "Reckon you know that. There's too damn many Indians around."

"Aim to try," Rye said curtly. "Now head for that brush to the south of us."

Immediately Wilkinson cut his horse about and pointed him in the direction Rye had ordered. The lawman, on the alert, pulled in slightly behind him while Dixie, also close, brought up the rear.

Both the yelling and the rifle fire had lessened. There was only an occasional shot breaking the relative quiet. Fuel had been tossed onto the fires which now blazed anew. Apparently the invaders had been driven off. They were making their escape just in time, but they still needed to take care. Riders were yet milling about in the murky night, some Kiowas, others renegades. Spurring forward, he slapped Wilkinson's horse smartly on the rump.

"Move out!"

Wilkinson cursed and rocked back in the saddle from the sudden motion from the big white's quickened pace.

"Got to make it to that brush!" the lawman added.

In that same instant four riders swung in on them from the left. Kiowa braves, Rye guessed. Blocking the way, rifles leveled, they brought the lawman and the two with him to a halt. One raised his hand, pointed back toward the camp and barked something in a staccato string of words. Rye turned to the outlaw, anger and frustration gripping him.

"What's he saying?"

"For us to go back to the camp or they'll kill us right here." Wilkinson cursed as one of the braves rode in close and began to tie his hands together again.

Rye shook his head and looked over his shoulder. The flare of the fires in the half dark showed where the camp lay. If they'd had only a few more minutes the attempt to escape might have been successful.

"Well, what about it, Mister Lawman?" Wilkinson bantered. "They got four rifles to your one. You aim to fight them? It sure don't matter to me. I figure I'm a dead man either way."

Rye's wide shoulders lifted and fell. "Turn around," he said. "We'll go back. Maybe we'll get another chance."

"I sure wouldn't go planning on it," Wilkinson said.

"One rule I live by," the lawman said as he surrendered his rifle to one of the braves, "I never give up."

Twenty

THEY RODE BACK to the Kiowa camp in silence, Rye
bitter at their failure to escape, Dixie equally downcast
and fearful. As to Hode Wilkinson, his attitude and manner had changed little. It was as if their ill luck at getting
free of the Kiowas had no meaning for him either way,
which indeed was the fact. Death on the gallows or at the
hands of the Kiowas offered poor choice.

They reached the camp and went straight to the tipi of
Talking Bird. The old chief, grim and arrow-straight, came
out to meet them as they pulled up. Elsewhere in the camp
braves were removing the dead, dragging the renegade
bodies off to a nearby arroyo where they were unceremo-
niously tossed into a pile.

The dead Kiowas were being accorded better treatment.
Braves were taking up their lifeless bodies and laying them
out in front of one of the tipis. Later they would be taken
back to the main Kiowa village for burial. The wounded
had already been cared for and were sitting in the center
of the clearing, their weapons still handy should it become
necessary to again use them.

Talking Bird spoke to one of the four braves who had

halted their flight. The man, still on his horse, turned away and rode to the gathering. One of the wounded warriors got to his feet and walked with a distinct limp to where the chief faced the captives. It was Little Horse, the lawman saw. They could expect no help from him.

The chief spoke again, this time to the remaining three riders, two of which wheeled away in a stirring of dust and joined the men in the center of the clearing. While they were moving off, the last of the quartet dismounted. With his rifle still leveled at the prisoners, he took up a stand beside the chief and Little Horse who were carrying on a rapid conversation in their native tongue. When they finally finished, the latter turned to Rye, who, like Dixie and Hode Wilkinson, was still on his horse.

"Chief Talking Bird asks why you tried to steal our prisoner and escape with him. Were you not treated well?"

"That is of no importance. One Ear is my prisoner, and not the prisoner of the Kiowas. We are that way now only because you make it so."

"Talking Bird will not bargain words with you! This is Kiowa land."

"Is it not Arapaho land? Are you not trespassing?"

"No, the Arapahos do not claim this country. It is hunting grounds of the Kiowas. Talking Bird felt kind toward you and your woman. He was to let you go on back to your people when we reached our village. But now his thoughts are different. You have betrayed his trust."

Little Horse paused. He was breathing heavily. Apparently he had been wounded in the fighting, but was too proud to admit it. The lawman looked more closely at the brave. A dark stain of crusted blood was barely visible under the gray shirt he was wearing.

"Talking Bird says that now you must go with us. You are unworthy of trust. Therefore you will be our prisoners and we will return to our village. There Talking Bird and the elder chiefs will decide what is to be done with you."

Indians respected courage and bravery. Rye drew himself erect in the saddle and faced the old chief. He needed to put on a bold and fearless front if he and Dixie, and hopefully Hode Wilkinson, were to come out of the confrontation alive.

"Talking Bird and the elder chiefs will bring bad trouble down upon themselves and the Kiowa people by holding us prisoner. It will be wise to free us now."

Rye glanced around. Most of the Kiowa braves were now in the center of the camp. Some were eating, and all were talking excitedly as they relived the attack by the renegades and the subsequent battle. The lawman centered his attention on the brave standing beside Talking Bird. He looked tired and several times glanced toward the crowd in the center of the clearing as if wishing he could join them.

"We do not fear the soldiers," Little Horse said. "We have overcome them before."

"Our soldiers are stronger than ever. Many Kiowas will die if they oppose them."

Anger flared across the brave's face. "Such will not be true. You will go with Lame Horse to the tipi where you were placed. One Ear will be taken to—"

Rye's hand had moved to his side and down into his boot. His fingers wrapped about the bone handle of the knife he carried there. Half turning, as if to comply with Talking Bird's order, he started to move off ahead of Lame Horse. In one quick twist he was out of the saddle and on the ground. His hand came up, the blade of the knife he was holding catching and reflecting the light from the nearby fire. In the next moment he had the blade pressing against Talking Bird's throat.

"Tell that brave to give his rifle to my woman or I'll kill Talking Bird," the lawman said in a low, grinding voice. "I'll kill you too, if you yell."

Little Horse stared at the marshal. His deep-set, glittering eyes were nearly invisible in the uncertain light. Rye pressed the blade harder against the old chief's withered neck. At once Little Horse spoke. He passed Rye's order on to the brave holding the rifle. Begrudgingly the man handed the weapon to Dixie. Rye cast a quick look at the gathering in the center of the clearing. It was still in progress; no one had noticed the exchange taking place in front of Talking Bird's shelter.

The lawman motioned to Little Horse. "Now, you and your friend—Lame Horse I think you called him—get in the chief's tipi. I'm taking him with us. If any of you follow you'll have a dead chief."

"A Kiowa does not fear death."

"Maybe not, but does Talking Bird want to die for One Ear?" Rye glanced again at the gathering. The braves were still occupied with eating and talking, but the lawman knew that would not continue much longer. Once the braves knew what was taking place, they would be down on him and the others in a solid body, and all hope of escape, of even staying alive, would be gone. He pushed harder on the knife.

"You want to be the one who caused your chief to die? Decide quick, Little Horse. I have no more patience."

Little Horse shook his head. Jaw hard set, he said something to the other brave. Both turned and started for the chief's tipi. At that Rye nodded to Dixie. Pointing to the rifle she was holding, he said, "Keep that on Wilkinson. I don't want him trying to get away."

As the young woman nodded, Rye threw another quick look toward the center of the camp. There was still no change, but he knew each moment decreased their chances for escape. He touched the arm of Talking Bird, who stood rigidly beside him.

"You ride with me," he said, motioning for the old chief to mount the buckskin.

Haughty, Talking Bird moved his head slightly. Coming about, he swung up into the saddle. Rye kept close to the man to prevent free movement on his part, and climbed up behind him. Never for a solitary moment had he removed the blade from the older man's throat. Settled, free hand grasping the buckskin's reins, he took a final look at the braves gathered in the center of the clearing. They were still unaware of what was taking place.

"Move out," he said quietly. "Go slow. Head for the brush again."

"We ain't going to get far with that old brave holding us back," Wilkinson said sourly as they started slowly off into the shadows. "Cut his goddam throat and dump him."

"Keep riding," the lawman replied. The braves were still gathered and showed no sign of having noticed their departure. Little Horse and Lame Horse were yet in the chief's tipi and had set up no alarm. Rye knew that, too, would not last. They could even at that moment be cutting a slit in the rear of the canvas shelter and getting loose.

"Move faster," he called softly to Wilkinson, who was in the lead. "Need to get to that brush before the rest of the Kiowas realize what's going on. If we don't make it and they spot us, you know what'll be waiting for you."

Wilkinson immediately quickened the pace of the big white he was riding. Rye then turned his attention to Talking Bird. He had not once removed the knife from the chief's throat, but now, with a hundred yards or so separating them from the camp, the lawman slacked off. He

doubted any of the braves in the clearing would hear
should Talking Bird yell. The danger lay now in Little
Horse and the man with him sounding an alarm.

But it would be necessary to halt soon. He had to tie up
Wilkinson, now riding without any ropes restraining his
movements. That he could not trust the outlaw was, of
course, a foregone conclusion, and the sooner he got a
rope on the big mountain man the better.

They rode into the brush. Wilkinson slowed and looked
back.

"Keep going," Rye said.

They were still too close to the Kiowa camp, and he
needed to rid himself of Talking Bird as soon as possible,
for, as Wilkinson had said, the chief's presence was slowing them down. That moment was not yet at hand. With
the need to put the outlaw back in a rope and the possibility of the Kiowas already being on their trail pressing him,
the lawman continued on for another mile. There he
called a halt.

"I reckon it's safe to turn you loose about here, Chief,"
he said, and pushed the Kiowa leader from the saddle.

Talking Bird went to the ground, rolled, and came to his
feet. Rye gave the man a brief look, saw that he was un-
hurt, and riding up to Dixie, took the rifle from her.

"Go on!" he shouted at the outlaw, and pointed to their
right.

Talking Bird would be watching them. He'd let the old
chief think they had struck off west. As soon as they had
put a respectable distance between them and where they
were leaving Talking Bird, he'd cut back east. In the dark
he doubted the Indians would be able to track them.

Twenty-one

GRUMBLING AND CURSING, Hode Wilkinson cut right into the brush. Dixie was immediately behind him, trailed by Rye.

"Do you think they're following us?" the young woman asked as she freed a thorny branch that had caught on the leg of her trousers.

"You can bet on it," Rye replied, looking back to the north. A faint yellow glow in the night from the Kiowa fires marked the camp's location.

"I don't hear anything—any yelling," she continued doubtfully.

"You won't," Rye said. "And when you do it will be too late."

"These rawhide strings on my hands are too damn tight," Wilkinson complained. "They're a'cutting right into my—"

"Keep riding," the lawman replied. "You can stand it till we stop."

A quarter hour later Rye changed directions, turning completely around and setting a course due east. He was not exactly certain where they were as it was unfamiliar country, but the move was necessary. Searching Kiowas, directed by Talking Bird, would be prowling the area west of the brush; it was only smart to head the opposite way.

They rode on steadily, if slowly. The night was dark and there was no trail to follow. It was simply a matter of making their way through the undergrowth, picking what appeared to be the path of least resistance while staying on course.

Eventually they broke out of the undergrowth and were again in fairly open country. Rye, his attention divided between Hode Wilkinson and the almost certain possibility the outlaw would attempt to escape, and the country to the left as well as behind them where he could expect the Kiowas to appear, called a halt in a deep dry wash.

"Stay in your saddle," Rye said to Wilkinson as he swung down. "Not aiming to worry about you any longer."

Wilkinson muttered, raised his tethered hands and rubbed at his jaw with the back of a wrist. He had worked at the rawhide thong until it was almost off. The lawman took note of that.

"Just in time, too," he said, handing the rifle to Dixie.

"Just what're you aiming to do?" the outlaw asked. "You ain't putting a rope around my neck again, are you?"

Rye merely nodded, and took the short, extra coil of hemp that he carried from his saddlebags. It was not nearly as long as the one he had used on the outlaw at the beginning of their journey, but he'd make it do. The original rope had been lost to the Kiowas when they took the outlaw from him.

"That'll sure make it hard to ride."

"Means nothing to me," Rye snapped, finishing a slip

knot noose at the end of the abbreviated lariat. "Bend over, toward me."

"The hell with you!" Wilkinson yelled, and threw himself off the saddle at Rye.

The marshal had only a fraction of a moment to jerk to one side but the mountain man's outflung arms were enough to knock him to his knees. At once Rye rolled away, came upright. He lashed out at the outlaw with the rope he had coiled in his hand.

Wilkinson cursed, and with a powerful effort, snapped the weakened rawhide cord binding his wrists. Cursing again, he lunged at Rye. Once more the marshal dodged to one side, outmaneuvering the larger, slower man. He dropped the rope, and as Wilkinson surged in, drove a balled fist into the man's jaw.

Hode slowed, staggered slightly and shook his head. Whirling, arms extended, huge hands spread, he came on. Rye darted to the side again. He had put everything he had into the blow to the outlaw's jaw and it had scarcely fazed the man. Again he avoided Wilkinson's rush, and once more smashed his fist into the outlaw's jaw. Again it had no visible effect.

Rye backed away fast, the sound of the mountain man growling like some huge animal in his ears. His heel came up against a rock. He fought to catch himself, retain his balance and escape the towering bulk of Wilkinson closing in on him. He failed, felt the shocking blow of the outlaw's fist smashing into the side of his head. He went down reeling.

Groggy, he rolled away instinctively, struggled to regain his footing on the uneven ground. As he came partly upright, Wilkinson closed in and drove another savage blow to his head. Lights popped and Rye's senses went into a dizzying spin. He staggered, fell backward, came up against Dixie's mare.

"John! John!" He heard her voice as if from a distance. "He's killing you! I'm going to shoot him!"

Rye's head was clearing slowly. He could hear Wilkinson cursing, could also hear him stumbling over the rocks as he came in again. Hitting the man with his fist was a waste of time and strength. He twisted about and raised his hand to the girl.

"The gun—give me the gun!"

Instantly he felt the cool metal of the rifle's barrel come into his grasp. Taking a side step to get away from the mare, he seized the barrel with his other hand. Wilkinson, rumblings coming from his throat, continued to move in. The lawman drew back the rifle, swung it with all the strength he could muster. He heard a crack as the weapon's hardwood stock connected with the outlaw's head. Wilkinson sagged and went to his knees as the rifle broke into two separate pieces.

Rye, still clutching the barrel of the weapon, staggered forward. Wilkinson was struggling to regain his senses and get back on his feet. Mercilessly, the lawman clubbed him again on the side of the head with the metal remains of the rifle. Wilkinson groaned, his eyes rolled back, and tipping sideways, the outlaw went sprawling onto the ground.

For a long minute John Rye stood motionless over the prostrate Wilkinson while his breathing slowed and became normal. Nearby Dixie had left her saddle and was hurrying up to him.

"Are you hurt?"

The lawman wagged his head slowly. His jaw ached from the blows the outlaw had landed, and there was still a ringing in his ears.

"No, I'm all right."

As his senses cleared, he looked around. The early pre-dawn light had strengthened and things had become more distinct. They were too much in the open, he saw, and at once he turned his attention to their back trail and to the area to the north. Relief moved through him. There were no signs of the Kiowas.

"Got to keep going," he said in a quick, tight way, tossing the remains of the rifle aside. He was again without any weapon other than his knife. Even the old trap-door loading Springfield would be welcome.

"What can I do to help?"

Rye pointed at Wilkinson. "Need to get him tied up before he comes to. Have you got any stout cord or rope in your saddlebags?"

The young woman turned hurriedly to the mare and searched through the leather pockets hanging from the saddle. She glanced at Rye, shook her head.

"No, nothing."

The lawman made no comment but retrieved the rope he had dropped, stepped over to the unconscious outlaw and placed the loop he had fashioned about the man's neck. Then he removed the length of rawhide Wilkinson was using as a belt, and pulling his hands together, tied them tightly, making certain there was no slack that Wil-kinson could work at. That done, he began to slap the man vigorously to rouse him.

"Come on, Hode, wake up!"

The outlaw stirred. Rye put an arm about the outlaw's thick shoulders and endeavored to get him back on his feet.

"Get up, Hode! I want you back on your horse. The Kiowas'll be showing up pretty soon."

Wilkinson muttered something unintelligible. He half

turned, pulled himself upright. As he swayed back and forth, senses still hazy from the blows the marshal had delivered, Rye took him by the arm, guided him to the white and helped him up onto the saddle. His head was clearing slowly at that point, and as he settled into the hull, he stared at his bound hands in a dazed sort of way.

"Ain't right," he mumbled. "You can't treat a man this way." Reaching up, he touched the side of his head carefully. "What did you hit me with?"

"That," the lawman replied, pointing at the shattered stock of the rifle and the barrel lying nearby.

Leaning over, he wound one end of the rope around Wilkinson's left ankle, passed the remaining length under the white's belly and looped it about the right. With the loose end in his hand, Rye crossed to the buckskin and anchored it to the fork of his saddle. He started to mount, hesitated, having second thoughts about the shattered rifle. The barrel would serve well as a club. He slid it into the saddle scabbard and climbed onto the buckskin. Dixie was already on her mare and waiting.

"How far are we from Cimarron, Hode?" he asked, once more looking to the north and to their rear. It would be folly to think the Kiowas were not hunting them.

The outlaw shrugged. He was still nursing the side of his head. "Hell, I don't know! A far piece for damn sure! When you going to get me something to eat? I ain't hardly had nothing for a couple of days."

"We've got some pemmican the Indian girl gave us. Chew on a piece of that. How far to Cimarron?"

"Go to hell," the outlaw muttered. "Just you find your own way to Cimarron."

Rye's jaw hardened. "Reckon I can do that. Maybe take a bit longer, and that rawhide won't get no looser."

Hode spat, stared at the lawman. "All right. Follow out this here draw till it comes to a canyon. Be a trail there. Heads south. Stay on it. Leads to Cimarron."

"How far?"

"Couple of days—all depending."

"On what?"

"How many Indians catch up with us, and when. You ain't even got a gun so's you can't put up no fight."

Rye admitted that to himself, but he did have his knife and the rifle barrel to use as a club. He'd had mighty hard luck with weapons on this trip. First the shotgun lost in the saloon at Brimtown. Then his .45, and then the extra pistol he always carried in his saddlebags for emergency, both taken by the Indians.

The rusty old cap and ball Colt slipped to them by Morning Sky had been useless. The 45-70 Springfield rifle which would have served its purpose was taken away by the Kiowas, and the good lever action he had obtained after overcoming the brave back in the tipi was now in ruins. The lawman shrugged; a man couldn't have much more bad luck than that. But he guessed he'd manage somehow. He nodded to Dixie.

"Give me a couple of chunks of that pemmican. We'll make it do until I can snare a rabbit."

Dixie dug into her saddlebags and came up with the requested bits of shredded deer meat and fat.

"Here," Rye said to the outlaw, and tossed him one of the portions. He glanced at Dixie. "Where's yours?"

She shook her head. "I don't think I want—"

"Better make yourself want it. Been a time since we had something to eat, and it's hard telling just when we will again."

The young woman gave that a few moments' thought,

and then took a thin strip out of the cloth in which it had been wrapped.

Rye nodded and smiled tightly. "Maybe we can do better before the day's over. Just keep your eyes peeled for a rabbit—even a deer."

Twenty-two

FOLLOWING THE DIRECTIONS Hode Wilkinson had given him, and verifying that they would take them south according to the sun, if not to Cimarron, Rye headed his party off down the draw. Going directly to the settlement did not matter as much for the time being as moving in the right direction. He knew the Santa Fe Trail lay southward, and once they had intersected it he would have no trouble reaching the town.

They pressed on, making fairly good time as the brush had thinned and they had left the draw and were passing through a sparsely forested area of pines, small oaks and an occasional piñon. It was difficult to remain hidden with so little good cover, and Rye knew that the Kiowas, if they were somewhere in the vicinity, were certain to catch sight of them. But noon came and there was still no sign of the braves.

"Do you think the Indians have quit following us?" Dixie wondered when they had stopped beside a small creek to water the horses and rest for a few minutes.

"Doubt it," Rye said with a shake of his head. "They want Wilkinson too bad to do that."

The marshal had not released Wilkinson but let him remain in the saddle. Taking one of the canteens refilled with fresh water, he handed it to the outlaw.

"That what you figure, too?" Rye said.

"What's that?" Wilkinson said, taking a swig from the canteen.

"That the Kiowas won't give up chasing you."

The outlaw helped himself to another drink from the canvas-covered container and passed it back to Rye.

"Sure do. They ain't about give up on me." He turned about and looked to the north. In the nearby trees several jays were quarreling over the juniper berries that had fallen to the ground.

"I owe you, Marshal," he continued. "Them redskins would've had me peeled and roasted by now if you hadn't tricked them and got me loose."

"Just saving you for the hangman," Rye said dryly.

"Maybe so, but you won't get no more trouble from me. I know which side of the bread the butter's on. I'm better off locked up in jail than back there hogtied by them Indians, or that bunch that raided them."

Wilkinson paused, looked off into the distance. His wide, thick shoulders stirred. "I can bust out of a jail. Done it plenty of times, but there ain't always a chance you can get away from a bunch of redskins—unless some help comes along."

"They get their hands on you again it's not likely you'll get away."

"Ain't going to bet against that, but there's one thing I'm damn sure of, Marshal."

"Yeh?"

"You go ahead an' put me in jail, and then once I bust out I aim to hunt you down and pay you back good for

hitting me with that rifle. I figure I owe you for that. Ain't
no man ever—"

Rye smiled. "If you've got it in mind to pay me back, as
you say, for doing what I'm paid to do, you'll have to get
in line. There's a string of others ahead of you with the
same idea." The lawman nodded to Dixie. "Best we move
on."

At once the young woman turned to her horse and
climbed into the saddle. She was tired, worn out, that was
apparent to the lawman, but they dare not rest yet.

"We'll make camp soon . . . when dark comes."

Dixie shrugged. "I'm all right."

They moved off, and came soon to a rocky slope. Rye,
hoping for such, cut east. If the Kiowas were tracking
them the hard surface of the long slope would reveal no
tracks and hopefully confuse them.

"That there sashaying around ain't going to fool them
Kiowas none," Wilkinson said some time later when Rye
resumed a southerly direction. "Them rocks'll slow them
down a mite but not for long."

"Maybe for long enough," Rye said. "You know who
that bunch was that raided them?"

"Some. One of them was a Mex vaquero name of
Gomez. Seen a couple of Comanches and two or three
white men. Rest was Mex bandidos, all Comancheros, I
reckon."

"Renegades all of them," Rye said. "What would they
be after? That wasn't even a Kiowa village. Nothing for
them to take."

"Horses," Wilkinson said. "Horses and women, but I
reckon they got this bunch of Kiowas mixed up with some
other one because they sure didn't have no women along
'ceptin' yours and the gal, Morning Sky."

"We owe thanks to her for helping us escape," Dixie said, "and for this—this meat we're eating."

"Hell, she's a Indian," Wilkinson said. "I don't figure I owe her nothing."

"Was it the Kiowas that killed your folks?" Rye wondered.

"I ain't sure, but it don't matter none. Redskins are all alike."

Rye made no comment. Wilkinson's hatred for all Indians was apparent. He glanced back. They were well below the rocky slope they had angled across and were now following out a narrow arroyo.

"You're wrong there, Hode. The tribes aren't all alike and all bad. Goes for the whites, too. They're not all good or all bad. Both kinds are running loose in this country."

Wilkinson turned his head and spat. "I sure ain't come across no good Indian yet!"

"Probably because the ones you've run into know you for what you are and how you feel about them."

"I ain't never tried to hide that," Wilkinson said. "Got me to thinking. I know them critters and I figure we ain't seen the last of them yet. You're sure going to need some help and I'm real ready to give it to you."

"It's mighty comforting to hear you say that," the lawman replied dryly.

"I mean it! They jump us again, you cut me loose I'll find me something to fight with and maybe we'll all come out of it with our hair."

"Obliged to you, Hode," the lawman said, "but I expect I'd make out better without you."

The day wore on, growing warmer as the sun climbed overhead, and then a few hours later becoming cooler. They would need a fire that night, the lawman thought, and as the shadows began to lengthen, he began to look for a suitable place for a camp, one that would provide them protection of some sort from the searching eyes of the Kiowas.

A steep-walled canyon offered the best solution. The trail they had been following lay a distance to one side, and the entire area was thickly overgrown. They would not find a better location. Continuing along the trail for a short distance to where a rock slide had all but wiped it out, the lawman turned off and backtracked for a half mile or so before returning to the canyon. He doubted the ploy would fool the Kiowas for long, expert trackers that they were, but it could throw them off until daylight, and by then he expected to be gone.

They made a dry camp in the heavy brush at the foot of the canyon's east side. There was no pressing need for water. They had two full canteens, and the horses had been watered a few hours earlier. Too, there was no food to cook even if they had the wherewithal to do so. Dixie did find some wild onions back up on a small flat and harvested a hatful, so the meal that night was one of pemmican, wild onions and water. It fell far short of satisfying their hunger but Rye and Dixie felt it was better than no food at all.

As for Hode Wilkinson, off his horse and securely tied to a tree, he grumbled and cursed as he ate his share, and had no trouble falling asleep shortly after.

Dixie, hunkered before the small fire Rye had felt was necessary, drew her jacket closer about her body to ward off the chill setting in. They were in high country where cold comes quickly after the sun sets.

"Is it true what you said about a lot of outlaws waiting their chance to kill you?" she asked, her eyes fixed on the flickering flames.

The lawman shrugged. "Goes with the job."

Dixie's features were serious. "It must be terrible for you knowing that there are men out there just waiting for the chance to kill you—shoot you in the back or something."

"Never think about it. When one of them shows up all cocked and primed to kill me, I'll do my best to kill him first, and that's exactly what I'll do unless the good Lord has decided my time has come."

Dixie shivered either from what Rye said or from the cold. "I—I don't see how you can live that way—just going day by day, or even hour by hour, all the time expecting some outlaw to show up wanting to kill you."

"Like I said, I never think about it, just keep my eyes peeled for trouble and be ready for it if it comes."

"But living your life that way—with death always so close—"

"Yes, I reckon it's that way, but like the Indians say, only the rocks live forever . . . Now, try and get some sleep. Got to make it to Cimarron by dark tomorrow if possible."

Dixie nodded, watched Rye get to his feet. "What are you going to do? Will you be close by?"

Rye detected the concern in her voice. "Figure to sit right here by the fire. Got to scare up more wood first. You crowd in close. Not saying you won't get cold but you'll make it through the night because I'll keep the fire going."

The lawman smiled reassuringly at her. She drew her jacket closer about her shoulders and lowered her head as he walked off into the dark night in search of firewood.

Returning with an armload of limbs and branches, Rye dropped them near the fire and turned to Wilkinson. The marshal had not been taken in at all by the outlaw's declared preference for jail or his offer to help in the event they were attacked, and he wanted to be certain the mountain man's bonds were secure. Examining them closely, he found them all to his liking, and choosing a place by the fire near Dixie, he sat down with his back to a rock, prepared to spend a not too comfortable night.

Morning came, cold and windy. Rye piled more wood on the fire and roused Dixie and Wilkinson and made ready to move out. There was no breakfast to be had so they mounted at once. Wilkinson was surprisingly cooperative in getting into the saddle and allowing himself to be tied to his horse.

They rode on a half hour or so, continuing to follow the arroyo's trail. They still had seen no sign of the Kiowas, due no doubt to the dense brush and stunted tree cover in the wash, but Rye did not relax his vigilance. Admittedly he was not too versed in the ways of the Indians, but he could not believe the Kiowas would give up on recapturing Hode Wilkinson. Too, he and Dixie were now most likely in the same wanted category as the outlaw. Not only had they taken the outlaw from the Kiowas, they had also humbled their chief.

"You going to stop along here somewheres and see if you can scare us up a rabbit or two?" Wilkinson asked later in the morning. "This here's a good place to find them—and I'm sure hungrier than all get-out."

So also would be Dixie, the lawman thought, and he was no better off. He looked about. They were in a grassy swale with considerable low brush. Likely there would be plenty of the small mammals around.

"Pull up over there by those rocks," he said. "I'll see if I can scare up a couple."

"I can help with putting out snares," Dixie said. "Zeb showed me how to—"

Rye lifted his hand for silence. He pointed to a small cluster of trees not far ahead. Three Indians sitting slackly astride their ponies had stopped and were discussing something. They were too far away for their voices to be heard, but by their many gestures the lawman reckoned the subject was of considerable importance. They had not noticed Rye and his party but the marshal was taking no chances. Cutting sharply right, he rode in behind a clump of juniper growing along the edge of the clearing.

"Kiowas," Wilkinson muttered. "Means there's more of the danged scalpers around close. What do you aim to do now, lawman? Cut and run?"

"Not likely," Rye said, tying Wilkinson securely to a tree. "Best thing we can do is just sit here."

"I know what I'd do if I had me a rifle," the outlaw said. "You ain't doing nothing?"

Rye waved the outlaw to silence. The trio of Indians had split up and were heading out in different directions.

"One's coming this way," Dixie said in a low, tight whisper. "What can—"

"Don't move—just stay quiet," Rye answered, slipping out of the saddle to the ground. He carefully drew the rifle barrel from the scabbard. To allow it to scrape against the leather could alert the brave.

Judging the point where the Kiowa would pass the clump of junipers, Rye eased forward. He could see the brave, hunched on his pony, head swinging from side to side as he searched the brush and rocks for the escaped prisoners. His two companions had already disappeared.

Somewhere back in the brush a grouse called. The Kiowa stopped, turned his attention in that direction. After a few moments he came on. Rye, holding the metal part of the carbine by the barrel, crouched lower and waited. The brave, if he did not change directions, would pass by little more than an arm's length away. Again the grouse called, the sound lonely and melancholy in the hush.

The Kiowa drew near. Rye tensed, both hands gripping the rifle's barrel with the flat mechanism forward to serve as a club. The brave slowed, his attention drawn to something off to the right. He was a young man, dressed only in breechcloth, moccasins and a headband. Sunlight shone on his skin and the muscles of his superb body shifted gently and smoothly as he moved. A fine-looking young man, Rye thought, but an enemy who would kill him as readily as he would a deer or some other animal.

The moments dragged by. Again the Indian moved on. Rye, set and ready with his iron club, felt sweat collecting on the taut muscles of his back. He glanced skyward, attention briefly claimed by a hawk moving swiftly overhead as it plunged earthward toward a prey. In the next moment the brave was directly before him.

He had a glimpse of the man's startled eyes, of his open mouth as he started to yell when Rye swung the rifle barrel. It caught the Kiowa high on the chest and partly on the neck. The pony shied, reared, spilling its rider to the ground. Rye lost no time at all, but sprang forward, ready to use his club again. The brave, quick as a bobcat, bounded to his feet. The lawman struck once more, this time laying the rifle's heavy part across the Indian's skull. The brave groaned, collapsed in a heap.

Snatching up the man's rifle, he gave it a quick glance and groaned. It was another old Springfield, trapdoor loading model such as had come into his possession earlier, but it was better than no weapon at all. Rolling the brave onto his back, Rye ripped the pouch of bullets

from his shoulder and wheeled to Dixie and the outlaw.

"Got to get out of here fast," he said in a tight voice.

"And go where?" Wilkinson asked.

"Head back the way we came. The main party of Kiowas is probably in front of us."

Twenty-three

CROSSING to where Hode Wilkinson sat tied to the tree, Rye bent down and hurriedly freed the knots. The outlaw stretched and chafed his hands.

"Hell, Marshal, how many times do I have to tell you I ain't going to try to get away? I'd sure rather be locked up in a cell than have them red devils working me over." The lawman made no answer. The rope loose, he stepped back and gave the length of hemp a jerk.

"Come on!" he said urgently. "I don't have time for you to do any lollygagging."

Dixie was already in the saddle, he noticed, as he helped the mountain man mount. When Wilkinson was seated, Rye tied the man's ankles together in the usual manner.

"And there ain't no use of that, either! I keep telling you—"

"I know what you keep telling me," Rye snapped. "It don't mean a thing!"

The lawman turned to his buckskin, quickly fastened the end of the rope that attached to the outlaw to his saddle, and then swung up onto the gelding. Pointing to a faint trail leading south, he cut about.

"Follow that. It'll be faster traveling," he said to Dixie.

They moved out at once with her in the lead, followed by the grumbling Hode Wilkinson. Rye, the old Springfield loaded and ready, across his lap, brought up the rear.

The day was strengthening and the night's chill had faded. Birds flitted about in the brush and twice they saw wild turkeys roosting in the top of the small oak trees.

"You could shoot one of them," Wilkinson pointed out. "Sure would beat that grease we been living on—and you ain't had no luck finding rabbits."

Rye looked over his shoulder. It was hard to believe they had encountered only three of the Kiowas.

"One shot and we'd have the Indians down on us before I could pick up the bird."

"Expect they'll be doing that anyway," the outlaw said. "Long ride to Cimarron, if that's where we're headed."

"Cimarron will do fine—but so will any other town we come to that has a good jail."

Wilkinson made no comment at first, and then stirring, shifted his large bulk on his saddle. "Way I see it we'll be mighty lucky to get anywhere with all them Indians running loose," he said and lapsed into silence.

They kept to the faint and seldom used trail, now only a narrow path winding through the brush and trees. Occasionally they broke out into open country where they had only the hollows and dips between low hills to conceal their passing.

Around midday they came again to a fairly deep arroyo, one that served as a drain for the higher plains as well as the lower area when they were hit by one of the wild, furious thunderstorms that periodically visited the land. Sage, buckbrush, wild berry and prickly pear cactus grew plentifully along the arroyo's floor. Junipers, small oaks and piñon trees could be seen here and there but mostly it was a barren strip of country.

Rye was not comfortable with it and waved Dixie and his prisoner on, urging them to travel as fast as possible. A mile or so ahead he could see a band of larger trees thrusting out from the mountains well to the west that would provide good cover. It would be several hours, however, before they could reach that point.

Not long after noon Rye killed a rabbit with a rock, and when they stopped an hour or so later to rest the horses, he skinned the cottontail, built a low fire and roasted the small animal. It was the first good food they'd had but he did not waste much time on the meal. He was soon in the saddle and hurrying on.

"Ain't no need of this," Wilkinson complained. "We could've stayed put right there, killed a couple more bunnies and took time to cook them done. This starving is sure getting me down!"

"You'll do more than starve if the Kiowas catch up with us," Rye said.

"Reckon I know that, but I ain't scared none. Man only dies once."

"But I hear the Indians know how to drag it out for a long time."

"Yeh, you're right. You're mighty all-fired set on getting me to a jail, ain't you, Marshal?"

"What I was sent here to do," Rye replied.

"Sort of spoil your record if the redskins got me first, wouldn't it?"

"Maybe, not that it would matter all that much."

"Well, you best start planning on it because I don't figure them redskins'll ever let you get to where you're aiming to go."

That they were traveling in the right direction was all

that mattered for the moment to John Rye. If they ran into trouble as Wilkinson continually prophesied, and which he himself anticipated, they would at least be closer to their destination and the possibility of help than if they were caught farther east or west.

"We'll get there," Rye said firmly, more to ease Dixie Oliver's mind than to assure Wilkinson.

Late in the afternoon they reached the spur of trees. Rye felt much better although there had been no indication the Indians were even in the area—a fact that puzzled him.

Had they given up their desire to capture him, make him pay for his misdeeds? It didn't seem likely. Rye doubted the Kiowas would forget what he had done so quickly. Maybe his earlier efforts to throw the braves off their trail, send them searching to the east, had succeeded. The lawman was not too familiar with the Kiowa tribe, but judging by those he did have knowledge of, the likelihood of the Kiowas giving up was very remote.

"We camping here for the night?" Wilkinson asked as they wound their way through the trees and lesser growth. "I'm hurting plenty. Being all trussed up like you've got me has got my legs to aching."

"Some time yet till dark," Rye said. "You can hold out for a couple more hours."

Rye would have welcomed a halt just as he knew Dixie would, but he felt it was necessary they get as far from the country where the Kiowas were carrying on their search as possible. Too, the nearer they got to the Santa Fe Trail the better their chances of running into not only travelers who could aid them but soldiers from Fort Union who regularly patrolled the route.

"Now, you get this rope off me and I'll show you how to catch up three, maybe four rabbits so's we can—"

The outlaw stopped speaking. Two riders had suddenly

closed in on them from either side. They were not Indians, but roughly dressed, bearded white men, clearly some of the outlaws that roamed the area preying on pilgrims. One rode in close to Dixie. He reached out and seized her horse's bridle.

"Now, just what've we got here?" he said, grinning broadly.

Rye brought up the old Springfield, quickly pulled back the big hammer and without any preliminary conversation drove a bullet into the outlaw.

Dixie screamed as the man fell sidelong into the mare. She thrust out her hand, pushed the lifeless body away and allowed it to fall to the ground.

Hastily flipping back the loading gate of the rifle, the lawman shoved another cartridge into the chamber. The second outlaw was staring at him, his mouth pulled down into a crooked smile.

"You sure oughtn't to have done that, mister," he said. "Old Tanner weren't much but he was a friend of mine."

Rye threw himself to one side as the outlaw triggered his weapon. The bullet made a clipping sound as it missed and cut a narrow path through the brush. The lawman saw another rider break into view. How many more outlaws were in the party? he wondered. Whirling, he handed Dixie the rifle and the sack of cartridges. He jerked the lead rope to Wilkinson's horse free from his saddle and jammed its end into the fork of the mare's saddle.

"Follow the trail!" he yelled, turning to face the outlaw levering the action of his rifle.

"I'll catch up—"

Dixie moved off as Rye lunged into the brush close by. The outlaw fired but Rye was moving fast, dodging in and out of the clumps of brush. He had drawn his knife and was trying to get in behind the outlaw or else near enough to the man he'd shot to seize his weapon.

"What the hell's going on here?" he heard the man who had just ridden up ask.

"Some jasper, I reckon he was a lawdog, shot and killed Tanner. Blowed him right out of the saddle."

"I seen a woman and a fellow on a big white horse a'running down the trail. That part of them?"

"Yeh."

"Where's this here lawdog you said was around?"

"He's ducking in and out of the brush. Had himself an old single-shot army gun. I'm waiting for him to show hisself so's I can plug him."

Hunched low behind a thick clump of rabbitbrush, the marshal gauged his chances for reaching Tanner's rifle, snatching it up and firing it twice before the two outlaws could cut him down. Slim, practically none at all, he concluded. He needed to come up with another idea.

Two Indians rode into the small clearing. Both Kiowas, Rye thought, but he wasn't sure. Evidently they had heard the gunshot and come to investigate, but had misjudged the location. One of the outlaws shouted, whipped up his rifle and fired. The bullet knocked one brave off his horse. His companion triggered his gun in almost the same moment. The bullet went true, found its target in the outlaw.

As the echoes rolled and smoke floated across the small open area, Rye, keeping close to the ground, crossed quickly and seized the rifle Tanner had dropped. Levering a cartridge into the chamber as he rolled, he snapped a shot at the third outlaw, who had leveled his weapon at the remaining brave. The bullet, hastily fired, struck the outlaw high in his arm. Rye triggered the weapon again, and muttered a curse as it clicked on an empty chamber.

The bearded man yelled. Reflex action tightened his finger on the trigger of his gun, still pointed at the Indian. The lead slug missed by several inches, and the brave wheeled his pony instantly and disappeared into the trees and brush. The outlaw also turned about, and clutching his upper arm with his free hand, vanished into the dense growth.

There would be more Indians nearby, Rye was certain. And there could be other outlaws. Roving bands of renegades, a product of the war—now over for more than a decade—plagued the trails of the frontier and provided an ever present danger for travelers on the main routes as well as the lesser ones.

Moving quickly to where Tanner lay, Rye dropped his empty weapon and took up the outlaw's rifle and a sack of cartridges with a nod of satisfaction. It was a lever-action piece and looked to be almost new. The outlaw was also armed with a pistol, a bone-handled Colt, commonly known as a "peacemaker," that rode high in the holster.

Rye unbuckled the belt, and resetting its pointed tongue in one of the many holes punched in the leather, slung it about his neck *bandolero* style. He was well armed now, although the rifle was a .44 caliber and the handgun a .45. But that didn't trouble him; he had plenty of ammunition for the latter.

Going to the buckskin, which had shied off into the brush when the shooting began, he mounted hurriedly and turned onto the trail. Dixie, with Hode Wilkinson, could not be far ahead.

Twenty-four

FOR THE FIRST HALF MILE or so Rye rode hard, weaving in and out of the trees as the trail cut its way through the congestion of growth. Branches brushed his arms and raked across his face, all of which attested to the fact the trail was seldom used. But it was not difficult to follow even in the lateness of the day.

He didn't believe Dixie and Hode Wilkinson would be too far ahead as they would be traveling much slower than he. A disturbing thought came to him. Could there be more outlaws along the trail? The third one he had encountered after the shootout with Tanner and his friend had noticed Dixie and Wilkinson's departure, yet he hadn't been inclined to go after them. The odds were better than good that there were other outlaws.

That belief brought a grimness to his hard-cornered face. Low over the buckskin, he spurred the horse to a faster pace. There could be other Indians in the area, too. He need be doubly watchful—and careful. He reined in the buckskin. He'd best go a bit slower, even forsake the trail and keep more to the brush. Rye wasn't sure why a caution had come over him suddenly, but he accepted it just as he did all hunches and inner warnings.

Now off the path, the buckskin necessarily moved much slower. The lawman, hunched in the saddle, the newly acquired .45 in his hand, maintained a constant vigil of the area through which he was passing. He was feeling a tinge of regret for what he had done. He wished now he had thought of some other course than sending the young woman on, forcing her to accept the responsibility for his prisoner. Forcing someone else to shoulder his duty wasn't something John Rye would ordinarily do. But in this case he was so determined to bring Hode Wilkinson to justice that he had unconsciously put necessity first, and the consideration of whether it was right or wrong, last.

He could hear nothing, nor were there any untoward odors such as those of a campfire or tobacco to give warning. But there was something digging at his mind. There was something wrong, he was certain. Holstering the pistol, he drew the rifle and laid it across his lap. Twice his stealthy passing frightened deer and sent them bounding off through the trees. Birds fluttered in the brush and frantically rushed off at his unexpected appearance. And at each incident Rye jerked to full expectant alert.

That was not to his liking. He was much too jumpy, like a skittish horse. Why? He'd been through worse before. He pondered the disturbing question as he rode on. Was it that he feared for the safety of Dixie Oliver? No doubt that was a factor. Was it for the outlaw Hode Wilkinson, and the possibility the man might somehow trick the young woman and escape? Or was it that he feared the Kiowas and their resolute stubbornness to take the outlaw from him—a process that would mean harm to Dixie?

Abruptly he brought the buckskin to a stop. The distant sound of a man's harsh laugh had come to him from somewhere ahead. He rode out a long minute, and hearing no more, continued slowly. The smell of wood smoke reached him. Shortly afterward he saw the pale glow of a campfire among the trees. Again he halted. He'd be better off on foot. Dismounting, with the rifle in the crook of his left arm, his right hand grasping the reins of the buckskin, he moved forward cautiously.

"You boys just cut me loose and I'll make you a good deal."

It was Wilkinson's voice. Evidently Dixie and he had been stopped and were being held by outlaws. Their captors were not Indians, otherwise Wilkinson would not have spoken as he did. Rye pressed on in the deep brush. The flare of the fire grew. There was more coarse laughter. Rye halted, wrapped the lines of the buckskin about a stubby but stout clump of buffalo berry. Hunched low, the lawman made his way quietly toward the fire.

"Ain't but one good reason for grabbing you and that's for that there horse you're a'riding."

"You're forgetting the woman that roped him."

Rye paused briefly, drew his .45. With it in one hand, the rifle in the other, he moved on.

"You just do what I'm asking and I'll take you up to where the pickings are real easy. The law don't ever get there—and it ain't only pilgrims, but gold."

"Gold?" a different voice sounded quickly. "Heard there was some around here somewheres but never was able to find out just where."

"Mines've all been worked out around here from what I've been told," the first voice commented. Rye studied him through the screening brush. He was a thin-faced man with a tall, pinched crown hat.

"I ain't talking about mining, talking about finding nuggets in a creek—some as big as a hen's egg." Wilkinson's voice was strong, convincing.

Where was Dixie? The marshal's narrowed eyes probed the camp. Four outlaws—hard cases—in all. Bewhiskered, roughly dressed and apparently well armed. They squatted about the fire, were passing a bottle between them. Wilkinson, still on his horse, was off to the right. Dixie Oliver was nearby. A rope around her slim waist pinned her arms to her body.

"Nuggets?" one of the outlaws echoed. "Well, now you're talking my language! Just whereabouts is this here creek?" He was a younger man wearing a checked shirt among other odds and ends of clothing.

"Way back up in the mountains—a couple or so days' ride from here," Wilkinson replied in an anxious tone. "You take this rope off me and I'll take you right to it."

There was a long pause. Finally one of the outlaws picked up a wrist-thick branch and tossed it into the flames, shaking his head.

"Hell, I ain't about to swallow that! Nuggets big as a hen's egg—that jaybird's lying through his teeth! He's just trying to talk us into turning him loose so's he can make a run for it."

"Abe's right," another of the outlaws agreed. "This country's done been picked over good. Won't be no gold laying around just waiting to be picked up like he claims."

"Them's my sentiments to a tee," another of the outlaws said. An older man in parts of a faded blue uniform, he had remained silent during the conversation to that point. "I'm for getting out of here, taking his horse and the woman, and heading back to the Strip. That big white'll bring a mighty good price—and I sure could use some female company."

It was clear the outlaws were among those who holed

up in an area called the Strip, a panhandle section of Indian Territory some called Oklahoma. There was no law
in the area, and their kind could come and go in relative
safety.

"Reckon we all could, Charlie," Abe said. "Best thing
we can do is mount up and head east."

"What about the rest of the bunch—Tanner, and Ben
and Kansas? Ain't we going to wait for them?" the
younger outlaw asked.

"Hell, no! They're all full growed and twenty-one. Can
look after themselves. Anyway, when they don't find us
here I expect they'll line out for the Strip, too."

Rye's grip on his .45 tightened. He would have to do
something quick if he were going to save Dixie and his
prisoner. At the moment the men were fairly well
bunched; once they got up and prepared to leave they
would separate, and it would be hard to cover them all.

Moving quickly and quietly, John Rye stepped up to the
edge of the small clearing. Abe was the first to see him.

"Who the hell—" he began and reached for his gun.

Rye silenced the outlaw with a bullet to the chest. He
was never one to shoot a man down in cold blood, but he
was up against odds here and was not about to take a
chance at such a time.

"Rest of you—throw your guns into the brush! And put
your hands up!" he called out in a hard, direct voice.
"Make a wrong move and you're dead."

The outlaws got to their feet slowly. Carefully drawing
their weapons, they tossed them into the dense growth
nearby.

"He's done killed old Abe!" Charlie muttered, stunned.
"Killed him for sure."

"You want to do something about it?" the lawman

asked softly, pushing his advantage to the limit. "I'm right willing to accommodate you."

"Just who the hell are you?" Charlie asked.

"Name's Rye. I'm a U.S. Marshal. That man on the white horse is my prisoner."

Over beyond the three remaining outlaws Dixie had come to her feet and was pulling at the rope they had put around her. The gag that had been over her mouth had apparently come loose earlier and was now down about her neck. Wilkinson, slumped disconsolately in his saddle, looked on but said nothing.

"Now, we ain't done nothing, Marshal," the older outlaw said. "We was just camping here when the big fellow and the girl showed up."

"Why'd you put a rope on her?" Rye demanded. "You could see he was her prisoner."

"Well, we for sure didn't know what to do. We wasn't sure it had to do with the law, no, sir—we sure didn't."

"Well, it did," Rye said, imitating the man's drawl. "Might say she was acting as my deputy. Now step over there and take that rope off her. Any of you try to leave you'll end up the same as your friend Abe."

The outlaw crossed hurriedly to Dixie's side. Rye watched closely as the man drew a knife from his belt sheath and cut the rope. As it fell away, Dixie, a smile lighting her face, hurried to Rye.

"I prayed you would come, but I was afraid for you back there! There were three of them and—"

The lawman shrugged. "It all worked out fine," he said and handed her the rifle. "Keep them covered," he added in a clipped voice. "I'll get your horse and bring Wilkinson over here. Shoot if you have to."

Dixie smiled tightly. "That will be a pleasure after some

of the things they said to me. I'll be right happy to put a bullet in any of them."

"I can understand that, but don't do it unless you're forced," Rye said as he turned away. "The Kiowas are still around—probably close."

Dixie nodded and watched Rye as he circled the fire to where Wilkinson was sitting his horse. He took up the lines of the girl's mare and then those of the big white. Leading them, he returned to where Dixie waited, then, after ground-reining them, he brought up his own mount. Taking charge of the lead rope attached to Wilkinson, he nodded briskly to Dixie.

"Mount up."

There was an urgency to his tone, and stepping quickly to her horse, she went up into the saddle.

"What about us?" the outlaw called Charlie asked plaintively. "There's Indians around here. You just leaving us here?"

"I've got no time to fool with you," the lawman snapped. "Soon as we're gone you can dig your weapons out of the brush," he said as he went onto the buckskin.

"But them Indians! They're liable to come along before we can—"

Rye's jaw tightened. "You won't have to wait," he said. "They're here."

Twenty-five

DIXIE UTTERED a small cry and crowded in close to the lawman. She was all right, he had noted earlier, but there had been no time to talk. He glanced hurriedly about. The outlaws were dim, half-crouched, frozen shapes in the dancing firelight. Full darkness had finally come and the half-dozen bronze-looking braves at the edge of the clearing were also barely visible.

Rye reached out, dug his fingers into the cloth bag of bullets Dixie had hanging about her neck. Gathering up a handful of the thick 45-70 cartridges, he faced the girl.

"When I yell, get out of here," he said in a low voice. "Go down the trail." He nodded to Wilkinson. "Stay with her—this time I'll be right behind you."

Rye swung away, opened his mouth and broke the taut silence with a yell that echoed through the night. As Dixie and Wilkinson turned, Rye threw the handful of cartridges into the fire.

A shout went up from the Indians. Rye, the .45 now in his hand, drove two quick shots into the ground at the feet of their horses. As dirt and other debris spurted up, setting the horses to shying away, the cartridges in the fire began to let go. Rye wheeled the buckskin about, headed for the trail. Two of the braves, recovering from their surprise, and ignoring the explosions in the fire, surged toward him. The lawman triggered his weapon again. One of the Kiowas flinched and veered off. The second pulled up short, all the while yelling.

The cartridges in the fire continued to go off, filling the night with sound, smoke and glowing embers. Rye glanced back as he reached the trail. The outlaws had taken advantage of the confusion to duck into the brush. There seemed to be more Indians in the clearing but because of the haze filling it he couldn't be sure. He raced on, and for a short time heard nothing of the pursuit he was certain would come. That the exploding shells and the three outlaws would be enough to keep the braves busy was too much to hope for.

Even as the thought came to mind he heard the hammer of hooves behind him. The braves were coming on fast. He bent lower over the buckskin and thumbing cartridges from the belt slung about his neck, reloaded the weapon he'd taken off the body of the outlaw, Tanner. He wished now he had the rifle. He could do more damage with it, but it was in the hands of Dixie Oliver.

A gunshot cracked from somewhere behind him. Rye twisted about. Two of the braves had pulled ahead of the others, and were closing fast. Hanging low off their ponies, they offered a difficult target. The lawman raised his pistol and fired a shot at the nearest. He took no aim, simply hoped to slow down the pair.

Two more gunshots rang through the night. His bullet had not dissuaded either of the Kiowas in the least. They were still coming on, firing as they did. In fact, they appeared to have gained on him. He triggered another shot as the buckskin rushed on. He should be catching up with

Dixie and Wilkinson, it seemed, but they were nowhere within sight or sound.

He looked back. There were three braves now, two riding abreast, a third slightly to their rear. He fired again. The bullet hit one of the braves more by accident than by design. The Kiowa drew up from the crouched position on his horse and began to slow.

Abruptly the buckskin broke out of the brush and trees and was in the open. Rye saw Dixie and the outlaw. They had halted by a mound of rocks to wait for him.

"Keep going!" he yelled as he drew near.

For answer Dixie, skilled from years of living in the wilderness and hunting game, raised the rifle she was holding and pressed off a shot. The Kiowa in the lead jolted, clutched at his pony's mane to keep from falling as the horse swerved to one side.

The girl coolly leveled the rifle again. As Rye slowed to join her and the outlaw, she triggered the lever action once more. The second brave yelled and began to pull in his horse. He rode alongside the trail for a short distance, swung around, rejoined his wounded partner, and side by side they headed back for the brush.

Rye halted beside the young woman. His usually stoic features gave way to a smile. "That was mighty fine shooting."

Dixie's shoulder stirred. She levered a fresh cartridge into the rifle's chamber. "Was easier than hitting a cottontail dodging in and out of the brush . . . Are you all right?"

"Not a scratch. You the same?"

She nodded, ducked her head at Hode Wilkinson sitting silently on his horse. "Same with him . . . Looks like you're going to deliver your prisoner all in one piece after all, Marshal."

Rye turned, looked toward the distant brush. It was barely discernible in the night, but the few stars that were out made it possible.

"I'm obliged to you for your help. If it hadn't been for you it maybe'd come out different." Holstering his weapon, he smiled. "Expect we'd best move on. We're right near the Trail, and those lights you see way off there is Cimarron." He paused, looked again at the line of brush. "Never can tell about Indians. They just might change their minds and come on after Wilkinson."

Dixie smiled as she crossed to the mare. "I think the two of us could handle them," she said, mounting.

Rye, serious as always when it came to his responsibilities as a lawman, shrugged.

"Maybe, but I don't aim to try," he said. "Never been much of a hand to push my luck."

The Man Behind the Book

"I appreciate my readers' loyalty. I've tried to never let them down with a second-rate story—and I won't."

No Western author has been more faithful to his fans than Robert Raymond Hogan, a man known as Mr. Western by Old West fans in over 100 countries around the world. Since the appearance of *Ex-Marshal* (1956), his first Western novel, Ray Hogan has produced entertaining Western stories of consistent quality and historical significance at a breakneck pace.

This prolific author's credentials rank him among the great Western writers of all time. Hogan's credits include 145 novels, and over 225 articles and short stories. His works have been filmed, televised, and translated into nineteen foreign languages.

"I'm a person with a great love for the American West, and respect for the people who developed it. I don't think we give enough credit to the pioneers who moved west of the Missouri in the early days."

Ray Hogan's ancestors first arrived in America from Northern Ireland in 1810. Commencing with his great-grandfather who journeyed from Pennsylvania to Kansas around 1825, losing his life to Osage or Pawnee Indians, the Hogan family history is one of western migration. His grandfather moved from Tennessee to Missouri, and his father began a law enforcement career as an early Western marshal in the Show-Me State before moving to New Mexico when Ray was five years old.

The wild frontier of yesterday is simply family to Ray Hogan. His lawman father met and talked with Frank James after the famous outlaw was released from jail, and once suffered a serious stab wound in the chest while bringing a train robber to justice. Ray's wife, Lois Easterday Clayton, is the daughter of a New Mexico family with its own pioneer heritage. Her grandfather began commuting between New Mexico and Missouri by horseback and stage in 1872 as a circuit-riding Methodist preacher "with a rifle across his knees." At one time he encountered the Dalton gang in Missouri.

Ray Hogan's boyhood was spent hunting, fishing, and riding horses in the New Mexico backcountry; observing all that was said and done on working ranches; and cocking an ear in hotel lobbies while railroad men, rodeo performers, townsmen, and cowhands talked about life on the range. It was only natural he decided to devote his lifetime to firsthand examination of the Old West.

Ray Hogan is a meticulous researcher, his investigations having taken him all over the West. An extensive personal library of books, pamphlets, maps, pictures, and miscellaneous data attests to his ravenous appetite for Western details. Throughout his intense, lifelong study he has painstakingly strived for authenticity.

Readers equate a Ray Hogan Western with excellence. His trademark is a good story full of human interest and action set against a factual Western background.

"I've attempted to capture the courage and bravery of

those men and women that lived out West, and the dangers and problems they had to overcome."

Ray Hogan still resides in The Land of Enchantment with his equally talented wife, Lois, an accomplished artist and designer. This outstanding American continues to deliver in a way unsurpassed by his peers, keeping the Old West alive for those of us who missed it.